The Twis
The Presiden
The Collector's Edition

The Twisted Case of the Presidential Conspiracy

Zeb Dasher Mystery Novels, Volume 2

Myron Baughman and Dr. Myron Baughman

Published by Myron Baughman, 2024.

This is a work of fiction. Similarities to real people, places, or events are entirely coincidental.

THE TWISTED CASE OF THE PRESIDENTIAL CONSPIRACY

First edition. October 7, 2024.

Copyright © 2024 Myron Baughman and Dr. Myron Baughman.

ISBN: 979-8227653703

Written by Myron Baughman and Dr. Myron Baughman.

Also by Myron Baughman

Pneumasites
Pneumasites 2

Zeb Dasher Mystery Novels
The Twisted Case of the Presidential Conspiracy

Standalone
Pneumasites
Educating Everett
My Puppy Theo
Trixie: The Pixie Angel
The Ghosts of Griswoldville

Watch for more at https://www.sermonaudio.com/source_detail.asp?sourceid=kingjamesseminary.

Also by Dr. Myron Baughman

Zeb Dasher Mystery Novels
The Twisted Case of the Presidential Conspiracy

Standalone
The Strange Case of the Missing Bridge

Watch for more at https://www.sermonaudio.com/source_detail.asp?sourceid=kingjamesseminary.

This Book is Dedicated to My Loving Wife Denise

A Zeb Dasher Mystery Novel
By
Dr. Myron Baughman

This Book is Dedicated to My Loving Wife Denise

Table of Contents

1. Releasing the Unknown
2. The Meeting
3. To London from Sir
4. A Pleasant stay in Geneva
5. On the Way to Tehran
6. Terror in Tehran
7. Miss Azalea
8. Safe in Harm's Way
9. Questions with No Answers
10. A Friendly Visit to Ukraine
11. Struggle in Russia
12. My Russian Welcome
13. Bumming It
14. An Evening Out
15. Our Adventure in Bagdad
16. A Captive in Iran
17. China
18. The Taiwan Connection
19. California Dreaming
20. Roaming in Rome
21. The Island of Despair
22. Playing Dodge the Bullets
23. Going on the Offensive
24. Investigating Royalty
25. Investigating the Investigator
26. Being Suicided
27. Paying My Dues
28. Finishing the Investigation

THE TWISTED CASE OF THE PRESIDENTIAL CONSPIRACY 3

Collector's Edition

1

Chapter One

Releasing the Unknown

The steel door opened, and two mental hospital men dressed in white stood in front of me. I have been in this nameless institution for many months, so many I lost count. I was never informed as to the location of this institution. I was placed here by my attorney as an option out from the maximum security prison. My stay in prison was a result of my last investigation, the Case of the Missing Bridge. Since I was considered mentally instable, and dangerous, I was kept away from other prisoners except for the once a week group therapy sessions. There were eight other patients in my group. We met in a large room on the second floor that always remained locked and guarded. There were steel bars at the windows along with wire mesh. All windows were double plated with unbreakable Plexiglas. There were always four guards on duty on my floor. I was never called by my name. I was only called 134,792 or 792 for short. I only had this identity since the prison assigned that identification to me. I am Zeb Dasher, internationally renowned crime investigator. I have solved cases that had been given up on many times. Now, I am kept here in this nameless institution for the insane because of what I had uncovered concerning our dystopian government. There were times that I had been kept in extended isolation. During these times, even I began to question my own sanity. It was dark days and nights for me.

"Come with us," one of the men standing in the doorway said to me.

It was not time for any session of any kind that I knew of, so something different was going on. I was led down the hallway by the two men, one on each side of me, to an office just on the other side of the door that opened to my floor. Inside there were three men seated behind one large desk, and one chair placed opposite of them. I was told to sit there, and wait to be questioned.

I sat in silence for around ten minutes, watching the men quietly confer with one another and compare notes. Then, finally, the man in the middle began to speak.

"You are 792, are you not?"

"That is how I am addressed," I replied.

"Why are you here, 792? Do you know why you are here?"

"I don't even know where here is, sir." I answered.

"All you need to know is that you are being held in a maximum security mental health facility as per the federal Justice System's decision made by the United States Attorney General. He has since then, left office. Now there is a new administration that is reviewing such cases as yours. Is that understood, 792?"

"Yes, so I am under review."

"Correct. We have some legal as well as psychological questions that we need to ask to make a proper assessment of your condition. After questioning you, we will make a recommendation to the Justice Department, and they will either release you, or bury you here."

"So, I am here for that questioning, or will that be held at a future date?"

"Today is the day. Therefore, you need to be honest with us, and answer all of our questions since all of them are important to the assessment. Do you agree to this, 792?"

"Yes, of course. Ask away."

The man on the left picked up the paper in front of him and asked,

"792, do you know the whereabouts of Clyde Ryner?"

"No sir, as far as I know Clyde Ryner doesn't exist."

"Yet, our intelligence reports that he was closely associated with you. He was a CIA agent who was last reported to be in pursuit of a Mr. Zeb Dasher. I don't know if you are aware of Mr. Zeb Dasher being wanted for questioning concerning missing CIA documents."

"That could be, sir, I am not sure about any of that. I thought he was a teacher, though," I replied.

"Do you know anything about the whereabouts of a Mr. Zeb Dasher?"

"Sir, yes I do."

"792, you are telling us that you know where Zeb Dasher is? Where would that be?"

"Zeb Dasher is sitting here in this chair, right in front of you. I am Zeb Dasher."

The three men became quiet then conferred with each other. In several minutes, the middleman spoke.

"792, we are afraid that you are still delusional. The evidence is in your last answer. We know for a certainty that Zeb Dasher is dead. He was drown in the Allegany River just north of Pittsburgh. There have been reports of people seeing him, but those have proven to be hoaxes. He is now only an historic legend as far as this committee is concerned."

"Well, gentlemen, you are all wrong. I am Zeb Dasher, and I am quite alive. Don't you have a record of my fingerprints? If you do, they match mine."

The three men conferred again, and again the middle man spoke,

"792, there are no records whatsoever of Zeb Dasher's fingerprints. He is a complete mystery to the Justice Department. To us, he is a legend that is all. He is about as alive today as Sherlock Holmes was. So, then, do you claim to be Sherlock Holmes as well?"

"If he is only a legend, then, why are you asking about him?"

"We are the ones asking the questions, 792. We only inquire of him to test your sanity, and you have failed."

"No sir, you have failed, not I. The man you refer to as 792 is indeed Zeb Dasher. Believe it or not."

The man on the right spoke up, "So, if you are this Zeb Dasher, what has become of the CIA documents that are missing?"

"Sir, those I gave to several reporters who published them in the newspapers. I also gave a copy of those documents to a friend of mine in the senate."

"So, 792, you no longer have the documents?"

"No I don't. You don't read the newspapers?"

"Yes, of course, but those reports in the papers have since been judged by the Justice Department to be phony misinformation. Only conspiracy theorists believe those reports." The man on the right replied sharply.

"Sorry, but it was not misinformation. It is just the feds are covering their tracks with their propaganda. It was all true, but they wouldn't or couldn't own up to it."

The man on the left spoke up, "So, what about Clyde Ryner? Where is he?"

"He is me, sir. He was just a phony identity that I had to use. I am an investigator, and I use many disguises and identities to get myself into places that I normally couldn't go."

"Like, perhaps, here, 792?"

"Not really. I am paying the price for some mistakes that I have made in past investigations of the super powerful. They have put me here to stop me."

"And who are these super powerful people, 792?"

"They are as nameless as I am. They are behind the power of the hidden deep, dark state that actually calls the shots world over."

"So, it's one large dark conspiracy, 792?" the man in the middle asked.

"Well, I wouldn't consider it a conspiracy, but a hidden shadow government. We don't elect them."

"Have you been reading about this 792?"

"No, I haven't read anything. I have experienced what I am talking about first hand, like the lawn fertilizer processing plant in Minnesota."

"Tell us about the plant in Minnesota, 792." The man on the left said.

"They use humans as part of the ingredients for the lawn fertilizer. When I got the word out to the press, they destroyed the plant."

"They? Who are they?"

"The puppet masters," I replied.

"I think we have heard quite enough, you may go back to your room now, 792," the man in the middle said.

I left with the two guards at my elbows. I had to stay in my room again without any further sessions of any kind for months. One day, my room door opened wide and to my surprise Rick Hasselton, my long time, covert CIA friend, was standing just outside the door.

"Zeb, you look awful. Get your shoes on, we're leaving here," he said. I noticed that there were no guards present in the hall.

"Rick! You are a sight for sore eyes!" I jumped up and jammed my shoes on in a hurry. I only had a white collared shirt and white pants on that the institute supplied to all their patients. That is what I wore out of there. Outside in the parking lot, Rick's sweet 1969 Charger 500, with the 426 high compression Hemi engine, waited for us. It was a thing of beauty and I was thrilled to ride in it once again. Rick wasted no time getting out of the parking lot.

"Now, that the unknown Zeb Dasher is free, there's a lot to do," I said.

2

Chapter Two

The Secret Meeting

"What is going on Rick? I mean what has happened that I am a free man all of a sudden?" I asked.

"You are free because you are needed, Zeb. Why should the foremost investigator that the world has ever seen be put away? Have you thought of that? Obviously, someone is hiding something. You have solved crimes that no one else could, Zeb. You cannot deny that. As to why you are free now I can tell you that there are some people, people with very big money, who want you to look into something for them. They bought off the government, so you are now free."

"Who are these people, Rick?"

"I can't tell you much, Zeb. My job is to just take you to them. We are going to Washington, D.C. to meet with the CC."

"CC? What is that?"

"The Clandestine Committee is what they are vaguely known as by the few that know about them. Not much is known about them except for the fact that these guys do not play around, Zeb, so this is serious business. Trust me, the governments of all the countries of the world listen to them. They freed you didn't they? Maybe, they can be considered part of the government, or the part that does the actual governing. I don't know. I am just not sure at this point."

"So, they want me to work for them? So, why are you picking me up instead of me getting a taxi or something?"

"My boss told me to take you to the committee, so here I am."

"Always the faithful soldier aren't you Rick?"

"Hey, I've been called worse. Do you know where you are at?"

"No, not for certain. This looks like south eastern Pennsylvania to me, but I'm not sure."

"Very good. They had you locked away in Pennsylvania all this time. You probably didn't have any clue as to where you were."

"No, all I ever saw were the high walls and sky above."

"I think you were probably in there for life, Zeb. I am glad you are out. Now if we can keep you out..."

"So, how close are we to D.C.?"

"We should be there in two hours or less. It depends on traffic. We will be going to the Hay-Adams next to Saint John's Church. That is opposite the White House, Zeb. Ever been there?"

"I've been to the White House, and all through it many times, Rick, but I never stopped in at the Hay-Adams. From what I understand it is quite nice."

"The Committee doesn't meet at a hamburger joint, Zeb. They go in style as jet-setters."

I settled back in the passenger seat of the Charger. Rick practically flew to Washington, D.C. He had the habit of aggressive driving, a habit that disturbed me sometimes, especially in congested areas. I decided to close my eyes and relax the best I could. I found myself falling asleep but Rick rudely woke me back up just outside the city limits. We stopped at a clothing store where he treated me with two new suits, underwear, and two new pair of shoes, along with a new suitcase. I was glad to get out of the white insane asylum clothing, and into something that I normally used to wear. I once again felt like myself. After that, we were off, non-stop to the five star Hay-Adam Hotel.

We pulled up to the front door and got out. A young man in a uniform took the key from Rick and went to park the car. The lobby of the building was fabulously rich looking. We went to the desk and were directed to go to the roof for our meeting. There was a snack bar on the roof that had a good view of the city, and especially the White House. The tables were rather small and round. Over to the one side of the roof there were several tables pulled around into a close semi-circle with one chair in the center. I realized that was where I was going to sit. The usher took us to the tables, and I sat down in the middle of the semi-circle. Rick sat down in a chair outside the circle. Soon, a group of six men was ushered to the tables. They all sat down facing me. We sat quietly for a while facing each other with very little movement.

Finally, one of the gentlemen spoke up. "Detective Dasher, we are here on very important matters, as you will soon see. You can refer to me simply as Mr. X. We have gained your freedom at considerable cost for a reason. We have questions that need answered. These are questions of the highest necessity to have solid answers found with proof. We are convinced that only you can bring about a faithful resolution to our problematic questions. You will be handsomely rewarded once you have completed your investigation for us. Are you ready for the details, Mr. Dasher?"

"Yes, please."

"This will not be an easy task being that it involves multiple tasks of espionage in the highest of places. The risk will be great. Secrecy will be of the utmost importance, Mr. Dasher. Do you understand?"

"Got it. Go on."

"We have reason to believe that the President of the United States is divulging top military secrets to the Communist Chinese and others. We believe he is receiving millions of dollars in secret overseas accounts through clandestine deals. As of yet, we have not been able to either track them or find them, if they exist. We have many financial ties the world over, and still we cannot come up with much of anything. This is where you come in."

"So, what makes you believe the President is a traitor to our country? Do you have any evidence of this, Mr. X?" I asked.

"It is only circumstantial, I'm afraid. Repeatedly, once a new system of weaponry or a defense system is presented to him, shortly after that, the Chinese have an almost identical system. They even have the new system when Congress hasn't approved ours, or it's still under construction. It is too often, for it to be coincidence. It is every time, without fail. It doesn't happen until the presentation to the President. We need to know just how they are getting these things. It appears to be unauthorized sales and shipments."

"Well, there could be any number of leaks in the development and procurement of a new weapons system, Mr. X. You should know that."

"I agree, but we have minimized the path with certain systems, and they don't appear in China until after the President is given access to the details. Then, some how they have the new system. We have one by one eliminated certain people from the privileged approval path, and none of them seem to be associated with the divulging the details of entire programs. The buck stops with the President, Mr. Dasher."

"I've heard that before. So, you expect me to track hidden money transactions that you don't know for sure even exist? You also expect me to delve into secret projects and track their information paths. That would mean a high security level for me to even attempt to look into any of this. I don't have any clearance in the Defense Department or White House at this present time, Mr. X."

"Precisely. If you choose to accept this assignment, we will send you to New York City to meet with Sir. He is our detail man. Sir will arrange things for you. You will receive the highest clearance in government, and an exceptionally generous spending allowance. If you refuse the assignment, you will be back in the mental institution by tomorrow at best. You will not have another chance to be released, ever. Now, Mr. Dasher, what will it be? The choice is yours."

"Wow, since you put it that way, Mr. X. I gladly agree to the assignment. Do I have a time limit?"

"Sir will give you more of the details when you see him. We have arranged for an appointment tomorrow in New York City at ten thirty in the morning. You will see him then. Mr. Hasselton will be your transport, but will not be involved in the meeting. Once he drops you off, you will provide your own transportation. Good luck, Mr. Dasher."

3.

Chapter Three

To London from Sir

"Here we go again, Rick," I said as I climbed into the car. It was a nice sunny day, perfect for a drive. New York City was not my favorite place to go, but it was business, so go I must. It is not a terribly long drive from Washington, D.C to New York, so we did not make any stops along the way. Usually, we will stop for a break and get snacks, but not this time. Rick seemed to be in a serious mood as he drove me there to the meeting with Sir.

"Listen, Zeb, this guy named Sir, I believe is a dangerous man. He seems to be part of what I consider the underworld. He is so rich and powerful, he is above international law. No nation will touch him even though he is nefarious in his doings. Politicians come and go at his bidding. People and groups disappear who offend him. I am telling you this so that you are careful as to how you even address him. You must be polite and positive. Thank him gracefully when the meeting is over. I know this may sound out of the ordinary, but this is not an ordinary man. Just be cautious, that's all."

"Am I supposed to bow before him and kiss his ring finger or something, Rick?"

"No, nothing like that. I just want you to stay safe.."

"That bad is it? What if I just don't go to this meeting? I'm free now, so why don't I just disappear?"

"Not a good option, Zeb, You would be better off dead when they catch up with you. Just go to the meeting and do what you are told. You will be compensated for completing your assignment. If you do not complete it to the committee's satisfaction, you won't be very happy.. So, just do your job. You do good work. I do my job as told. If I did not I would not be here driving this nice car, Zeb. The choice is yours."

"Well, drive on, Rick. Drive on!"

We arrived at the new Trump Tower on Fifth Avenue at ten-twenty. Rick wished me good luck and I went in the front door carrying my suitcase of new clothes. The lobby was large and spacious. I asked the woman at the desk as to what room I would find Sir, and she directed me to a small meeting room just off the lobby. I knocked on the double doors, and a man in a servant's uniform opened the door.

"May I help you?" He asked.

"I am here to meet Sir. I have an appointment at ten thirty."

The door closed momentarily and then reopened just wide enough for me to go in. The servant took my suitcase.

"Please have a seat in the chair on the left. Sir will be with you in a moment." The servant said walking me to the chair. I had a seat and the servant walked to another door and locked it. In a few minutes, two men with pistols in shoulder holsters came through a different door. They stood on both sides of a large, plush, velvet chair. A tall, rather elderly man with a short white beard next came into the room and stood in front of the velvet chair.

"Normally, my guests stand for me when I enter the room. I am Sir."

I promptly stood up and said, "Excuse me, Sir. I was not aware that you are Sir. Sorry, I have never met you. I am Zeb Dasher." I reached out to shake his hand, but he refused to raise his hand to greet me. Instead, he sat down in his chair.

"You may be seated, Mr. Dasher, so that we can get down to business. My time is valuable, probably more so than anyone else in the world. So, this meeting will be brief. I will tell you what I expect, and you will do it. It is just that simple. When you leave here, go to the JFK International Airport and board flight 685 to London."

The servant walked over to me and handed a flight ticket to me.

"In London you will meet with a Mr. Puckett, who will give you your credit cards to your Lloyd's of London account. Lloyd's is on Lime Street. We will have a car waiting at the Heathrow Airport to take you there. The plate on the black vehicle will end in the last three digits of 999, if you need it for positive identification. All of my vehicles have plates ending in 999. After you, leave Lloyd's you will then go back to Heathrow and fly to the Geneva Airport in Switzerland. There will be a man with a grey hat waiting for you at Gate B, the second gate. He will simply hand you a folder. That folder will give you credentials and the details of the mission in total. It will tell you where to go next. Do not deviate from your mission or from the details. It could cost you your life if you do so, Mr. Dasher."

The servant handed a second plane ticket to me, along with an envelope full of cash, and then unlocked the door. Sir and his two guards quickly left the room.

"A car is waiting for you just outside the front door, Mr. Dasher. Good luck," the servant said and handed my suitcase to me. The door locked behind me with a loud click. I hurried out of the front door to find a black limousine waiting for me. I climbed in the backseat, and it took off to the airport without me even saying a word. There I took my suitcase to the reception area and was given directions to where I could board my flight. It was quite a walk to the Delta staging area, but once there, I did not have to wait to board. I went right on the plane as a VIP and sat in seat A, the front executive section, upper deck of the 747. A stewardess took my suitcase and placed it in a cabinet at the top of the stairs. The stewardess told me that it would take six and a half hours to arrive in London, so that I should just relax and make myself comfortable. I had never rode in the luxury class of a 747 before, and found it very pleasant. I always was too money conscious to pay for the executive section. I ignored the movies that they offered, and decided to just lean back and rest for the entire flight. I was not sure about what I may get into later after arrival in London. I was not worried about it, since I planned on just following the directions that I was given to the letter.

We came into some turbulence as we approached the U.K. but landed without incident. I was handed my suitcase and I left out of the plane thinking it to have been a good experience for me. I walked out to the front of the airport and looked for a black car with a tag that had three nines at the end of the numbers. Amazingly, it was the first one I came to. Everything that Sir had told me about had worked out smoothly and without a hitch. That was encouraging. If the rest of the mission worked this easily, then the whole thing was going to be easy money.

I climbed into the back of the black car and it took me straight to Lloyd's of London on Lime Street. I got out of the car and went inside and asked for Mr. Puckett. I was ushered into a small office where Mr. Puckett was seated behind his desk.

"Mr. Dasher, I presume," he said and held out his hand to greet me. "I recognize you from newspaper pictures. You have been on television various times, once with the Queen."

"Yes, I am Zeb Dasher." I shook his hand, and sat down in one of the chairs.

"I have been expecting you. You are quiet a crime buster, world over."

"You could put it that way, Mr. Puckett."

"I'm originally from the states, Wyoming as a matter of fact. You are quiet a famous man, yes indeed. I had heard that you had died, though, some time back. That must have been some newspaperman's idea of a sensational headline or something." He chuckled. "Now, I am authorized to hand you this envelope," he said as he pulled a large envelope out of an unlocked desk drawer. He handed the envelope to me, and I opened it.

I pulled out one credit card with my name on them specially issued by Lloyd's of London.

"That card is unlimited," he told me. "It's called a Royal Gold Omega Card."

"Unlimited? What does that mean?" I asked rather dumbfounded.

"There is no limit on what you can spend on the card. It has infinite monetary backing."

"I never heard of such a card." I replied.

"Oh, they exist, only for an exceptional few. It has a magnetic strip on the back like all the others, and also the new chip on the front. Chips are for only these unlimited cards, so you may not have ever heard of a credit card chip. The American public probably won't see them in use there for twenty years, if ever."

"They are usable anywhere?"

"Any place on the face of the earth. Some places will take it over cash, or any other currency. Most places won't have a chip reader, except those that cater to the upper elite."

"Why is that?"

"That card is backed by gold, my friend, real gold, so don't lose it. It is not plastic, but is actually made of gold. If lost or stolen, call me immediately," Mr. Puckett handed me his business card. It had his personal phone number on it. "Day or night!"

He shook my hand and I left the bank with the card in my wallet and the envelope tucked under my arm. The black car was still waiting for me at the front door. I was impressed with that. I was then taken to the Heathrow Airport again where I boarded a flight to Switzerland for my international credentials. This was looking like it was going to be quiet an investigation; I just had no idea what was head of me.

4.

Chapter Four

A Pleasant Stay in Geneva

We landed at the airport and I got off the plane. Immediately, I saw a man with a grey hat standing at Gate B, the second gate, so I walked up to him expecting him to hand me another envelope. He did, but as soon as I took possession of it, two men came through the double doors of the reception area and ran straight at me. I took off running in the opposite direction with my suitcase and envelope.

This took me out onto the busy landing strip where planes were landing and taking off. They were hot on my heals, so I did not have much room to maneuver. A luggage cart came before me, and I hurled suitcases off of it at the men to slow them up. That helped a little. I was able to gain some distance from them. Suddenly I found myself facing an incoming passenger plane out on the landing strip. It was landing and coming straight at me. I looked back and the men were still in pursuit behind me, so I charged toward the incoming plane. I could hear alarms sounding all around alerting of eminent danger. Undaunted, I ran straight toward the huge aircraft. I knew it posed great danger to me. I could either be crushed by its many wheels or be sucked up into one of its powerful jet engines. This danger I knew also would deter my pursuers. It was an insane chance I willingly took. Quickly, the large front wheels approached me. At the last desperate minute, I leaped and rolled out of their reach. Coming to a stop, I lay flat on the pavement, hugging it for dear life. I heard one of the screaming engines pass over me, so I knew the danger from the wing was gone. I jumped up and ran again, away from the tail wing. The pilot had begun to turn the plane toward its unloading area. I looked back and my pursuers had run back toward Gate B and then disappeared into the crowd.

I decided to take a non-traditional exit from the airport. I walked off the tarmac, climbed a fence, and went to the street. There I was able to flag down a taxi on its way into the airport. He took me to a hotel that he personally recommended. Since I hadn't read the contents of the envelope that I had just received. I thought it best to get a room and freshen up before taking the next leg in my investigation, wherever or whatever that involved.

The cab took me to the Woodward Hotel. I paid the cab and walked in right past the doorman, carrying my own luggage. I walked up to the front desk.

"I need a room." I said.

"What is the name on the reservation?"

"Zeb Dasher," I replied, and the receptionist checked through his reservation book for my name.

"I'm sorry, but there is no reservation under that name. All of our rooms are booked months in advance, sir."

I pulled out my Royal Gold Omega Card and placed it on the counter. The man's eyebrows raised, and his mouth dropped open. He said nothing at first, then he began to sputter.

"I've seen a card like this only once before...a long time ago. Sir, if you will pardon me, I will check with the manager to see if there are any cancelations. Just a minute, please." He said and hurried to a back room. Soon, both he and the manager came to the desk with big smiles on their faces.

The manager spoke first, "Ah, yes, Mr. Dasher, I am Nigel Fried, there happens to be a cancelation that has just come open. It actually is our best penthouse suite. It has a wonderful view of the lake that all our royal guests like you just love! Would you care to look at it?"

"No, not at all. I'll take it on your recommendation, thank you. I would like to go and freshen up now, please."

The manager said with a huge smile, "Of course sir. Twiggs will see to your needs. And thank you for choosing the Woodward."

The manager shook my hand and went back into his office. Twiggs handed the sign in book to me, "Your personal attendant will be with you momentarily, Mr. Dasher." I signed the book and turned around to pick up my luggage and found that a young man in a nice uniform suit already had it in his hands. I looked around the lobby to get an idea of how good the hotel was. The lobby was immaculate and well decorated. They had many soft and comfortable chairs and sofas for the guests, several large front windows, and many expensive floor pots that housed various rare plants. I recognized one in particular that bloomed only once in twenty years. I was impressed. I was satisfied that this was a quality hotel.

"Sir, if you will follow me, I will take you up to your room," the young man said. He took me to an elevator and we went up to the top floor. The elevator stopped and opened up to a square hall that only had one door opposite the elevator. The attendant unlocked the door and opened it for me.

"This suite takes up the entire floor, Sir. If you have any needs presently, I will be happy to take care of them for you."

"No, not at this moment. Come in for a second."

We both went inside to the fabulous apartment.

"Everything is electronic, sir. There by the sofa you will find a remote control that operates just about everything in this suite. The curtains open using the remote, the large screen television, the bed, and the lights. You can even lock and unlock the doors remotely. If you need anything, press zero on the phone. That will go directly to the front desk."

"Nice. I could get used to this!" I said and put my suitcase on the sofa. I pulled out the one envelope that contained my cash and handed the young man a hundred dollar bill.

"Sir, my tips are included in my generous salary, so you don't have to do this," he informed me.

"Keep it, kid. I appreciate your kind help. I won't tell anyone."

"Thank you, sir," he replied with a smile and politely exited the room.

I took a shower, and settled on the plush bed to study my instructions that I received from the man with the grey hat. I put the envelope down on the bed beside my suitcase. I decided to comb my hair and then brush my teeth before I went any further. After I was done doing that in the bathroom, I came out and approached the bed. A cloud of floating sparklers strangely drifted through the air around the bed. I had never seen anything like it. Suddenly, I felt dizzy and ready to pass-out. There was something in the sparklers that was knocking me out. I backed into the bathroom to get my breath. The envelope on the bed could be seen to rise off the bed, seemingly by itself. It went waist high then disappeared. I thought I was delusional!

Then I saw it, a pair of eyes and part of a forehead floating through the air just above where my envelope had disappeared. I couldn't believe my eyes! I thought for a moment that my vision was distorted from the sparklers. Something invisible moved my suitcase on the bed also. Then, I realized someone was there at my bed. Somehow this person was invisible! As that person moved through the sparklers, I could almost see an outline of a human figure. Whoever or whatever it was, that person was intent on stealing my things.

I jumped from the bathroom door and tackled the invisible person. We crashed to the floor. In the struggle that ensued, I pulled what looked like a blanket off the individual. It was some sort of cloaking blanket, and a very good one. The man pushed me off, jumped up and exited the door. By the time I got to the door, he was already

THE TWISTED CASE OF THE PRESIDENTIAL CONSPIRACY

going down the elevator. He had escaped, but he had left behind a very valuable asset, the cloaking blanket. It was almost invisible on the floor, just a weak outline could be detected. My other possessions that he had picked up were lying under the blanket.

The man looked to have been Chinese. I had no idea how he even knew that I was in the apartment. He apparently was after the envelope with my final instructions. I still had my wallet also, so the man had failed to take anything. As soon as my head cleared, I called down to the front desk and complained that someone had gotten into my room and tried to rob me. The manager was shocked by the incident, claiming that the Woodward Hotel of Geneva had never had a robbery incident in its entire history. He told me that Twiggs, the front desk clerk, had reported that a man had ran out the front door a few minutes ago. He was on the security tape if I wanted to look at it, which I did later. I studied the tape, and memorized the face of the perpetrator. I suspected that he wore a disguise. I obtained a printed photo off the camera for my records. The manager offered the services of the house security, and the local police, but I told him that it wasn't necessary, since nothing was actually stolen. There was no explanation as to how the man had gotten into my suite. I figured that he had come in behind me when I first arrived. I definitely did not see him. I would have only known that he was there if I had bumped into him.

After all of that was settled, I sat back down on my bed. I opened the envelope and found several picture ID's and passports in it. One made me a top research scientist for NASA, Another showed me to be a special ambassador from the United States. My favorite packet showed my identification as a royal billionaire real-estate investor. One identity of interest was my identity as a member of the Taliban named Mohammad Ishmael. Another ID had me as a military investor who had billions to spend. I also found in that ID packet, eye contact lenses that changed my eyes from their being blue to brown. There were also small packets of hair coloring. In all there were seven different identities in the envelope.

I unfolded the short letter of instruction addressed to me. It read:

"Mr. Dash, by now you are in Switzerland, You will go from there to Tehran, Iran. There you are to find Abdul Abebe of the Iranian Revolutionary Army. Be wary of him, he is dangerous. You must obtain financial contact information addressed to and from the President of the United States or the Executive Office, as well as banking records. Abdul Abebe is linked in the pipeline that goes from the White House to China in a money-laundering scheme. He is a link to the Chinese leadership through Tehran, and is considered very dangerous. Signed, Sir."

I folded the paper and placed it back in the envelope. I then, put the envelope with all the ID's in an inside flap of my suitcase. I decided to rest in my beautiful suite for one day, and then leave for Tehran the following day. This was going to be a difficult assignment, if not impossible, so I wanted to enjoy my short stay at this fine hotel before embarking on such a difficult task.

After resting several hours I went down to the dining and lounge area on the main floor. I sat at a small single round table and ordered a ham and cheese sandwich for a simple snack. The waiter seemed amused at my order, but returned shortly with it on a fancy plate.

As I munched away on my fine sandwich, a beautiful, young Chinese woman, dressed in a glittering blue dress approached my table. She had long thick dark hair that reached to her shoulders and then did a slight flip.

"May I sit down?" she asked.

I stood up immediately, "Why yes, of course. May I order you something?" I asked as I helped her with her chair.

"Wine is all. A sherry will do."

My waiter came up almost as soon as she was seated. I ordered her wine, and sat back down, opposite her.

"I find Geneva so relaxing this time of year. I stop here even though I have no business ventures whatsoever here in this town." She said displaying a slightly British accent.

"I come here only on rare occasions. I stay too busy to just lounge like you see me doing today." I replied.

"It is good to relax once in a while. I try not to stress myself about things. What brings you to Geneva?" she asked.

"I have international business that I must take care of."

"International business? Well, that sounds interesting." She said as the waiter placed her wine on the table in front of her. "Is it terribly stressful?"

"No, I am skilled at what I do."

"Skilled? You must be an important man." She said and sipped her wine. "Skill is hard to find these days."

"Some may think so, others may think the opposite." I said taking the last bite of my sandwich.

"You have confidence, so I sense you are important in many ways. What kind of business is this international business, may I ask?" She said finishing her drink.

"Business between nations that involves billions of dollars, that is all."

"Well, Mr. Dasher, don't get into it too deeply. You will find it most unpleasant if you do," she said and stood up to leave.

"Thank you for that bit of advice, Miss..."

"Ching."

"Will I see you again, Miss Ching?"

"Not if you are lucky, Mr. Dasher." She said and walked away leaving the building.

5.

Chapter Five:

On the Way to Tehran

I walked out into the street to see where Miss Chang had gone, but apparently, she left in a waiting cab. It was a nice day, so I decided to walk down the street to take a brief look at the city. There were very nice store fronts that could grab anyone's interest. I stopped at what I would call a curiosity shop, named Graf's. When I walked in a little bell rang announcing my arrival. There were many porcelain antiques from all over the world. There was a large display of swords hanging on the wall, some looked to be very old. They had a nice counter of exceptional jewelry that I browsed over for a while. I contemplated purchasing something extravagant with my Royal Gold Omega Card, but it was difficult to decide.

"I am Mr. Graf. May I help you sir?" an old man wearing an apron asked as he approached me.

"I am just looking around for right now. I'm looking for something unusual."

"Unusual? Well, then may I interest you in this watch I have over here? It runs by battery, but you may want to operate the wind up stem for special occasions. When you wind it up and then press the wind up button in, it will shoot a wire out the top that uses the front watch facing as a hook. The wire is strong enough to support an average grown man. The more you wind it, the further it shoots the wire. It is a very unusual item."

"Wow, that is unusual. I'll take it. Does it keep good time?"

"Yes, it is set by the atomic clock in the U.K. "

"Do you have anything else that is unusual, like this?"

The man stood there for a moment thinking, "Why yes, come to think of it, how about a pen that fires the ball point out if you click it quickly three times in a row. It is a mini-weapon that you can put in your pocket. According to the instructions, its range is about fifty meters. I've never sold it to anyone, and it's been on the shelf for years. I didn't think anyone would be interested in anything vaguely dangerous."

We walked over to a wall that had shelving from the floor to the ceiling. The elderly man took a pen that was still in its original box off the shelf and dusted it off. "I thought about just throwing this thing out, but here, I'll give it to you if you want it since you are buying other things. Oh, yes, I forgot, it also records video. It really is an advanced pen. It's a bargain at no cost. Want it?"

"You are sure it still works?"

It's never been fired, sir, but according to the paper in the box, it is guaranteed to fire. It isn't reusable, that way, but will still write and record."

"Okay, and you are giving this to me?"

"Yes, I am an old man. I don't need this thing here."

"What else do you have that is really unusual? I mean, this has been great so far."

Mr. Graf walked over to his inventory leger and searched the pages. "Ah, here is one, you may like. How about a pocket handkerchief that can be used as a parachute? "

"Weird, but yes, bring that to me, and I'll buy that too."

Mr. Graf walked to a back room and came out with a handkerchief in a box and gave it to me.

"There you go. It will fit in your pocket. From what I understand it is made of super thin, non-porous material that expands when exposed to strong wind. It will stretch out so far for the parachute function but remain small in your pocket for the handkerchief function."

"Amazing,"

"Oh, how about a bullet proof vest, that doesn't look like a bullet proof vest. I have one of those in my clothing section next to the front window. Would you like something like that?"

"Of course."

Mr. Graf walked to the front clothing rack near the large window that displayed Graf's name to the public on the street. He came back with a reversible vest. One side was black and the other side was grey.

"You can wear it either way, both work the same. From what I understand these things are used by certain government agents in the U.K. who need subtle protection. It won't be effective against a powerful rifle but it will minimize injury from most hand guns. It even has pockets."

"Great, anything else?" I asked, pulling my credit card out.

"Perhaps not. I'd have to check my inventory sheets. I can't think of anything else for now. I don't have much in the unusual department. There isn't much call for such things."

"No, all of this is more than I expected coming in here. I just thought this was just another old junk shop."

"Old junk?" Mr. Graf smiled. "I hope you like your old junk."

He took the card and looked at it.

"Oh, I only take VISA or Master Card. I never heard of an Omega Card. It has no emblem on it, just this omega logo."

"It has a chip on it and a strip on the back, so stick it in your card machine and see what happens. You can't more than have to put this stuff back on the shelf. It's a universal card."

He ran it through the credit machine, then handed it back to me with a smile.

"It took it immediately. That is interesting. I learned something new."

"Your credit processer will be glad to process that card since it has the option of paying in gold. He'd be crazy not to take it."

"Gold? I never heard of that," Mr. Graf said and put my items in a decorated paper bag that had his name on it in fancy lettering. I left the little shop quite satisfied and went back to my penthouse suite on the top floor. I put the watch on my left arm, and looked at it. It was a nice looking watch. I went ahead and wound it a couple of times. I stuck my new pen in my shirt pocket, and tried the vest on. It was adjustable, so it fit. I sat back and watched some Geneva news on the television in my bedroom. I watched that for a while and then clicked through the various channels. I liked the television because it was a nice new one with a modern portable channel control that I could hold in my hand. My television back home was an antique compared to this model. I went to bed fairly early, since I planned on leaving the next day for Tehran. I didn't have a good feeling about going into Tehran, since they overthrew the American backed puppet government and set up an Islamic state. This was going to be an uncomfortable and dangerous assignment, but I knew I could do it if all went well.

Then the thought dawned on me that I had access to all this wealth, at least on a temporary basis, why shouldn't I use it to bluster my way through this mission? So, I went to the airport and bought a personal Gulfstream jet passenger plane, and hired a pilot, named Arthur, to fly it anywhere I wanted, and at anytime I wanted. I also hired four armed personal bodyguards who would dress in full military style uniforms and carry the best weapons and equipment. That done, I decided to visit Moammar Gadhafi in his home town of Sirte, Libya, before going to Tehran. Gadhafi would serve as a practice run for me before I presented myself to those in hostile Tehran. I would go as Palestinian sympathizer Mohammad Ishmael. This would perhaps keep me in good graces with the powers that be in both countries. I called Gadhafi direct using the hotel phone.

THE TWISTED CASE OF THE PRESIDENTIAL CONSPIRACY

"Omar, how are you dear friend, this is Mohammad Ishmael. Do you remember me? We met in Syria the time you visited. I'd like to see you tomorrow. My plane will land at Sirte tomorrow. Let's talk." I said.

"Mohammad Ishmael? I don't remember the name, but I will recognize you when you come. You are most welcome here in Libya. I will have a guest room ready for you my friend."

"Thank you, I have some things to discuss with you that I think you will like, See you tomorrow." I hung up the phone. I called down to the front desk and ordered a diamond bracelet to give as a gift to Gadhafi the next day. It arrived two hours later, in a beautiful gift wrapped box.

I wasn't sure what I would talk to Omar about the next day, but I probably could think of something by that time. I called my pilot and told him of my plans. We would leave at nine in the morning. I also informed my bodyguards who enjoyed staying with me in the luxury suite. They were treated like royalty by the hotel staff. As of tomorrow, they would become my "royal body guards." I also hired a man to act as my servant. I renamed him "James." All of my crew had very generous salaries that were at least three times the going rate, which would help keep them loyal. I would wear my contact lenses, and dye my hair dark for this mission. I phoned the desk and had them purchase a traditional Arab head garment called a keffiyeh. They brought it up to the suite for me in less than a half an hour. I was surprised at the speed of service that they offered. The young man who delivered it even showed me how to wear it. I told the manager that I would be leaving but I would retain my suite for as long as I wanted. It would be my home base. I would notify him if or when I wanted to discontinue my stay. He was fine with those arrangements.

The next day, I had one of my bodyguards help me dye my hair. It was almost black when we were done with it. I also put in my new soft contact lenses into my eyes. It took a little getting used to, but after a while I was able to forget that they were even in my eyes. I didn't need contacts but these seemed to help me with long distant things and I discovered later, they enhanced my night vision. I wore a black suit with my bullet proof vest and of course my keffiyeh. I looked to be Arab, or at least from the Middle East, but my speech would give me away. I decided to just say I grew up and was educated in the States. I couldn't disguise my voice with a phony accent and get away with it. There could be nothing phony about me, lest I give myself away.

We went to the airport where my pilot had the jet plane out and ready for me and my entourage. It was fueled up and ready to go. This plane had auxiliary tanks for international flights, so we could go non-stop. It was going to be an over sixteen hundred mile trip, taking about four hours.

Once we got to Sirte, we found that a white, stretched limousine was waiting for us. It took us to Gadhafi's fine palace. The limousine pulled to the front entrance where we were greeted by two of Gahafi's "Amazon" female guards. They escorted me and my servant James inside but my armed guards could only stand outside the front door. I was assured of my safety by "Cricket," the lead female guard. From what I could understand, she got the name from her long legs, and what she did with them. I didn't get into the details. Inside I was shown some of the luxury that the dictator enjoyed on a daily basis. Door knobs and all handles to drawers and cabinets were made of fine gold. There were several indoor swimming pools and hot tubs. The carpet was thick and plush. We were shown into a large white room that was totally decorated in white. The carpet looked as if it had never been walked on before. A very large white sofa lined three walls and had a long exquisitely ornate table placed to the one side. We sat down and waited for our host. It wasn't a long wait. Soon in came two men in uniform, who stopped and stood on each side of the door. They were followed by a man dressed in a much decorated military style uniform. He stopped at the entrance and took a hard look at me.

"You are?" He asked.

THE TWISTED CASE OF THE PRESIDENTIAL CONSPIRACY

James stood and said, "This, sir, is your friend Mohammad Ishmael, whom you have met in Syria."

"Oh yes, excuse me. I am so busy and I meet so many people that I do forget a name or two, but I do not recall the face. Maybe, it will come back to me later, but no matter." Gadhafi came over, shook my hand and sat on the sofa some distance from both James and me. "May I interest you in some drinks?"

"Well, not to be rude, but no thanks at this time. I'm still floating from the flight," I said with a smile.

Gadhafi smiled, "Yes, those long plane flights can be brutal. You are both American. I have a thing for faces. I never forget a face, and I don't remember you, Mohammad." He had suspicion written all over his face.

"Oh, that is understandable, I only was in a meeting with you in Syria, and met you in passing. I know you more from your reputation than anything else. Yes, I was born and educated in the United States. You are considered a friend and ally of the United States are you not?"

"Yes, that is true. I am an agent for the CIA. I feed them intel. But I feed them only intel that I want them to know."

"Of course, that is perfectly understood." I replied with a smile.

"So, then, Mohammad, what brings you my way for this visit? You had something for me?"

"Oh, yes, I do have something for you. A gift that I hope will bring you delight if you accept it. James, the box, please."

"Yes, sir," James replied, and stood. He pulled the gift box out of his jacket pocket and gently placed it in Gadhafi's outstretched hand.

"Oh, what is this?" He said with a delighted smile. He looked like a child opening a Christmas present when he took the lid off. "Oh that is gorgeous!" Indeed it was. The diamond studded gold bracelet was valued at one hundred thousand dollars, but I got it for only eighty thousand dollars because I used my gold card. He quickly placed it on his wrist. "Thank you. I will indeed wear this as a gift from my American friend." He sat and admired it for a moment.

"Think nothing of it. It is my privilege to give you what you by far deserve."

"So, then, you had something to tell me?"

Now, I came up with a story that I had made up the night before, It was pure fiction, little did I realize that it would actually happen. "My inside sources tell me that Lebanon will soon be bombed, and many U.S servicemen will be killed. There will be a retaliatory strike done by the U.S."

"So, do you have a date?" he asked.

"No, soon though. It's in the near pipeline. The word just hasn't been given yet."

"This is planned by the CIA?"

" The answer to that is obvious and doesn't need answered don't you think? " I replied with a smile.

Gadhafi smiled, "Strange, my friends in the CIA have not told me about such a thing."

"Like you said, they tell you the intel that they want you to know, and that is all. It works both ways."

Gadhafi smiled again. "I like you. Will you be staying long? My house is your house, my friend."

"Actually, no. I am off to the east. I have other friends to meet. I will be going to Tehran for a visit."

"Tehran? That is a rather dangerous place at the present time, and very Anti-American. I would hate to see you get into some difficulty over there."

"Do you have any contacts over there?"

"Yes, just a few. Some of them have been executed."

"Oh, that is too bad. I need to meet with their chief financial officer. I don't know who he is, but I may be able to offer him a good deal on American weapons, and military equipment."

"I don't know who that would be at the present moment. I will see if I can find out for you. American weapons? Indeed! Maybe, we could do business also." Moammar Gadhafi got up and left the room abruptly. He admired the bracelet on his wrist as he walked away.

We were escorted to fine bedrooms and slept well after they served us our meals. The next morning, Cricket gave us a message from General Gadhafi. It was the name of the head of the largest bank in Tehran. We were to see him when we got there. It was nine thirty when we were to leave the Libyan airport. Our pilot had been notified the night before and had our plane ready. It was all set to fly toward the rising sun.

6.

Chapter Six

Terror in Tehran

We took off and flew to Tel-Aviv as a short hop to our ultimate destination, Tehran. I had to promise my employees double their pay to get any of them to agree to go into Tehran. Two of the guards quit in Tel-Aviv, and flew back to Geneva. I couldn't actually blame them. Money isn't everything, especially if you aren't alive any longer to spend it. Then, there was the possibility that we may end up in some sort of prison. I had to count on my credentials to keep us safe.

We stayed in Israel long enough to refuel the plane and eat at the airport restaurant. Later that day, we landed at the Tehran Mehrabad airport and took a rental car to the Central Bank of Tehran at the NO.198,Mirdamad Blvd. My pilot stayed behind at the airport until further notified. There I left my body guard entourage standing on the sidewalk outside of the bank building by the rental car. Inside, James and I went to the front information desk and asked to see the Governor of the Executive Board. The name of the man who I was to contact was Mohammad [1]Farzin according to Gadhafi. Everyone there was dressed in western style clothing and looked like professional businessmen. I was the only one wearing a keffiyeh.

"I am here to speak to Mohammad Farzin, please,"

"Who may I tell Mohammad Khan is inquiring for a meeting?" the man at the desk questioned in English.

---

1. https://www.cbi.ir/page/22284.aspx

"Tell him that it is Mohammad Ishmael from the United States, and a friend of Moammar Gadhafi. I am here to inquire about an international business transaction."

"Please excuse me, then, I will do that personally." The man left the desk and disappeared behind a double door. Around the room I could hear people speaking in Farsi, so I didn't really get the drift of what was being talked about. Several people looked at me as if I were a curiosity.

"Agha-ye Farzin will soon be out of his meeting, if you care to wait, please have a seat right over there," the man behind the desk stated and pointed to a row of chairs to his left. I went over and sat down with James. As we sat, I noticed that a number of people began to stand around and look at us as if we were suspicious people. James began to be nervous. We were obvious strangers.

"You may see Agha-ye Farzin now. Come this way," the man at the desk said and motioned for us to follow him. We entered the door to a large office, where a young man in a business suit was seated behind an impressive desk. He stood up a raised his right hand,

"Come, sit down," he said and pointed to two chairs in front of his desk. I shook his hand and sat down. James quietly sat down without saying a word. "Mohammad Ishmael, what brings you my way?" he asked with a smile.

I showed him one of my credentials and said, "I represent a conglomerate of private corporations in the United States that manufacture and sell military weapons, hardware, and gear. We are interested in doing business with you, if you care to invest. We offer the best of everything to you, including low prices on package deals," I said.

"Package deals? What kind of package deals?"

"That would be groups of weapons if sold with supporting systems and long term promises to buy, we offer different package deals for the different kinds of weapons. There of course are the weapons in the nuclear field, the navy, ground forces, and air. I am here to see if we can strike up some sales interest on your part."

"Sir, I'm sorry, but I am not authorized to make such deals. You are badly mistaken. Those type of decisions go through other channels. I deal with the financial end of the decision, but don't make the decision to buy."

"That is understood, but our meeting is quite necessary from my point of view. We must know of other deals being made through U.S. government agencies, in particular the executive branch, so that there is no conflict of interest or undue waste on your part. In order to do this we would need a record showing what the U.S. is supplying both openly and covertly. Could you give us that record so that I may show my business partners in the states. Pricing and what is being sold is all important. We want to be competitive so that we can save you money. The money you save by dealing directly with us will be rewarding to both you and I. Could you supply us with such a report?"

Mohammad [2]Farzin sat at his desk for a moment, and then, stood up, "Yes, I could supply you with that information, but it will take a little time. I will have to make several phone calls, and the reports have to come from several different offices. My getting the reports for you depends on some red tape and several levels of administrative procedure. Are you staying in Tehran? I will call you at your hotel room when all is ready. I do this as part of the deal."

"Actually, we have just flown in and have no rooms yet. Can you recommend a nice hotel?"

"The Tehran Mehrabad International Airport hotel is the most convenient for you. I can call to see if they have a room available."

"That would be very kind of you. Yes, please." I replied.

The young man picked up his desk phone and made arrangements for me, Mohammad Ishmael and his entourage to stay the night. We rented a room for each one of my employees, so it was five rooms in total, including my pilot.

---

2. https://www.cbi.ir/page/22284.aspx

"There, you are all set. I will call you when the reports are ready. The hotel has modern services, so I will just send the reports over to you out of a courtesy. I look forward to doing business with you. Maybe we can make some money," Mohammad Farzin[3] said as he shook my hand and showed us to the door. He handed to me a business card with his name and several numbers on it. James and I walked quickly through the lobby of the bank and out to the front where my two bodyguards still remained. They had been questioned by the police, already, and were amazingly not harassed. Apparently, they were satisfied with a copy of my diplomatic paperwork that I had given the guards while we were yet in the plane. It proved in my mind that the paperwork that Sir, Mr. X, and the man in the gray hat had given me were authentic. We made ourselves at home at the airport hotel. It was a very nice hotel, but in the back of our minds, we were uneasy. We would all feel better once we were back in the air, headed back to Tel-Aviv. None of us left the hotel for any reason, lest we miss the call from Farzin. No call came that day.

The next morning we enjoyed a nice breakfast at the hotel dining area. Soon after breakfast, and we were back in our rooms, my room phone rang.

"Mohammad Ishmael? Yes, this is Mohammad Farzin. The sales reports are in, and I'm sending them over. You should be able to pick them up in the lobby in a few minutes. Thank you, and let me know what your investors decide as soon as possible. There are some interested military parties here in Tehran who are asking about it. Give me a call. You still have my business card don't you? It has my name and numbers with which you can get a hold of me. May Allah be with you, my friend." He said and hung up.

I thought his conversation ended rather abruptly for some reason. I called my pilot in the next room to go and get the plane ready because we were probably going to leave very soon. I then went down to the lobby, alone. I felt that there was no need for anyone to go along since

---

3. https://www.cbi.ir/page/22284.aspx

I was just going to pick up some more paper work. I walked up to the front lobby desk and asked if my paperwork had arrived from the Central Bank.

"Yes of course. Paper work for Mohammad Ishmael arrived just a few minutes ago." The desk clerk pulled a large envelope out from a drawer and handed it to me.

I thanked him and turned to go to the elevator when I saw a soldier standing immediately behind me.

"Excuse me," I said and attempted to go around him.

"Mohammad Ishmael?" he asked.

"Yes," I answered.

"I am Abdul Abebe, I am here, on behalf of the Iranian Revolutionary Army.to arrest you for espionage." The soldier pulled a set of handcuffs loose from his military belt. I knew I couldn't be taken captive by this regime. I would be in prison for life if not executed. I stuffed the envelope down into my pants. I then pulled my pen from my shirt pocket and pointed it at him.

"Is that how you treat diplomats here?" I said in a raised voice aiming my pen at him.

"Diplomat? More like spy!"

I quickly clicked the pen three times and the ballpoint exploded out of the rest of the pen and struck Abebe in the throat. I tucked the pen back in my pocket. I ran to a waiting elevator and went up to the fifth floor where my room was. When the elevator door opened, I saw soldiers standing by my door as well as at each of my entourage's doors. I closed the elevator door and went to the top floor. From there, I went to the roof. The door to the roof had a lock on it but it was only hooked on the latch, not locked. I ran out on to the roof, and pulled my handkerchief out of my suit pocket. I carefully unfolded it. On each corner of the handkerchief I found looping strings attached. I assumed that the user was to put their hands or fingers through the loops and hang on for dear life when using it for a parachute. It didn't matter, down below at the front of the hotel door I could see military men gathering. I walked to the other side of the building and from there I could see that my pilot Arthur had moved my jet plane near the airport runway. I decided to jump for it off this side of the building. My only hope was this handkerchief. My life depending on it working. The pen had worked, so I trusted the parachute handkerchief. This was different, though, my life depended on it. No more thinking, I went ahead and jumped, holding the handkerchief high over my head, and spreading it as wide as it would go. At first, I was in a free fall, but just after two flights of falling, the chute fully opened beautifully. I had a hard landing on the pavement, but nothing was broken. I stuffed the parachute into my coat pocket the best I could, and ran to the airport. By the time I got to the plane, I was quiet exhausted. Climbing in, I said, "Get this thing up!"

"What about everyone else?"

"We can wait a few minutes to see if they make it, otherwise we have to leave!" I said and we sat quietly watching out the plane windows. Then, out of the airport gates my two guards followed by James could be seen running as fast as they could. By the time they climbed into the plane, military men showed up at the gate, and ran toward the plane. We closed the doors and the pilot, Arthur, sent the plane down the run way. Suddenly a large international passenger plane could be seen coming down for a landing, heading toward us on the same landing strip as we were. Arthur turned the plane around in a hurry and then gunned the throttle. The jet engines screamed as we rushed down the run way just ahead of the oncoming passenger jet. The nose of our little plane came up just as the big passenger plane touched down behind us. We took off just in front of them. That was a terrifying escape, but amazingly we were all safe and on our way back to Tel-Aviv, and then, Geneva.

I then took the time to take my colored contact lenses out of my eyes. The hair dye would have to wait to be washed out at the hotel in

Geneva. Afterwards, I looked over the paperwork in the envelope, and from what I could initially tell, there were many transactions that were unapproved by Congress of military sales and shipments going to Iran, and many of them were going directly through the Executive Branch. Some were designated also to end up in China as per agreement according to the note at the bottom of one of the pages.

I looked out my passenger window and was shocked to see MIG fighter jets high up in the sky.

"Arthur, do you see the fighter jets up there?"

"Yes, I do. We haven't gained much in the way of altitude after taking off, sir. I've kept us low. Right now we should be flying under conventional radar. Those jets may detect us if they have look down radar, though. The pilots may spot us."

"They must be looking for us, Arthur, so keep us as low as you can."

"I'm bringing it down to just above tree tops, sir."

"Not too low, we don't want to hit a tower or something."

"If they see us, we are done. They will shoot us down for sure," Arthur said.

"May the Lord blind them!" We huddled in a quick, but sincere prayer together in the back of the plane, and then went back to our seats. We all sat anxiously in our seats, and steadily watched out the windows. After a long while, the jets disappeared behind us, and we safely made our way to Tel-Aviv with no further incidents.

6.

Chapter Six

Miss Azalea

By the time we landed at the Tel-Aviv Airport we had recovered from the heart pounding incidents that we went through in Tehran. We decided to rest a day in the city before traveling on to our next stop. If we went non-stop to Geneva, we would saving a lot of time. Since we were all anxious to rest safely in Geneva, I made the decision to go non-stop. Arthur recommended that if need be we could stop in Romania to refuel and have a break from flying.

While Arthur saw to the parking of the plane in Tel-Aviv, we made our way to the airport restaurants. I decided to eat at the King David Lounge in terminal number three while at the Ben Gurion Airport. We spent some time there just relaxing, chatting and enjoying some refreshments.

I was over at the donut bar when an attractive Chinese woman, dressed in an expensive looking, sparkling pink gown came up to me.

She smiled and asked, "Are the donuts fresh?"

"They bake them fresh here every day. My! Do you always wear fine dresses to airports?"

"Oh this little thing? I picked it up in Paris for practically nothing. I am here on a short layover to Geneva. I must meet my sister Ching there, well, she's my half-sister. My father died and my mother remarried before she had me. I am two years younger than Ching Ching."

"Interesting, to say the least. I've already met Ching in Geneva. Small world isn't it? I am on my way back to Geneva. I'll be leaving soon. I own a Gulfstream jet. I plan on leaving as soon as we are refreshed here in the lounge and my plane is fully refueled. We like to stop sometimes for a break from flying. It makes it more enjoyable. Anyways, I am anxious to get back to Geneva so we will be leaving very soon. It was nice meeting you," I said and turned to James and my two bodyguards behind me. Burt, one of the bodyguards, looked at me and frowned, shaking his head.

He came over to me and whispered into my ear, "Stay away from her. She looks like trouble."

"You are leaving now? Oh, can I hitch a ride with you? I'm afraid that I have two more hours left to my layover. I hate being stuck in these airports with all these common people. They smell. "

"Sir, we are pretty full," Burt said loudly.

"Oh, I don't weigh much, if that is what it is. I don't even need to take my luggage with me, I will go as I am. Just as long as I can get out of here. I'm tired of waiting. I can pick up my luggage at the Geneva airport later. They will send it on without me being on the plane, you know. So, please, will you give me a lift so I'm not stuck here?"

I looked over at my two body guards and James. James had an expression of disgust on his face.

"Well, I don't see any harm in it. There is enough room for you, actually. Chet, one of my body guards will accompany you to the plane and sit with you." I said. Chet rolled his eyes and shook his head.

Arthur came into the lounge and picked up two donuts and a drink, "Okay, we are good to go. The plane is fueled, and checked out. All that is lacking now, are my passengers." He smiled.

"Make room for one more, a Miss..., what did you say your name was?"

"Azalea, Azalea Ching, you may call me Azalea."

"Miss Azalea will be joining us in our flight to Geneva, Arthur. She will be escorted by Chet during the flight."

"Very good, sir," Arthur said and we all walked to the plane.

"This certainly is a spacious private plane!" Azalea said as she stepped inside. "Most private planes are tiny, but this is very roomy."

"Chet, show Miss Azalea a seat in the back. I'm sure she will find it to be comfortable there."

Chet escorted her to a back seat, and they both sat down.

"If everyone will strap themselves in, we will be lifting off in a moment," Arthur announced as he went into the front cockpit. He quickly ran through his final checklist, and moved the plane into position to take off. I sat in a front seat with James beside me, Burt was in the seat immediately behind me. Soon, we taxied into final position and I could hear the jets increase in power. I looked over at James and he was slumped over in his seat as if he were sleeping. I leaned forward and looked beyond James, and there stood Azalea with something in her hand.

I could feel the plane lifting off the pavement as I unbuckled my seat belt. Azalea lunged forward with a needle aimed at my neck. I dodged it and pushed her back. Once I gained the center aisle, I could see that everyone in the passenger compartment had been tranquilized. Azalea attacked me again, pushing with both arms the hypodermic needle that was in her right hand. I fell against the front door of the plane and it flew open. Azalea realized that I was about to be blown out of the door, so she released me. Desperately, I reached down and pressed the stem of the watch Mr. Graf had sold me in Geneva. I hadn't wound it much, but as soon as the stem was pushed in, the top exploded off, sending the facing through the opening between the plane door and the door frame. Apparently, the wire wrapped around the hinge of the door, because I found myself slammed against the outside of the plane, dangling by the thin wire attached to my left arm.

THE TWISTED CASE OF THE PRESIDENTIAL CONSPIRACY 51

My plane was still ascending and gaining speed. I knew I must get inside before long because it was very difficult to breathe. I could be beat to death against the outside of the plane. I pulled myself up the wire, one arm length at a time. I grabbed the edge of the door opening and pulled myself in. I saw Azalea on the floor attempting to regain her footing and I threw myself toward her, knocking her back to the floor. She picked up her hypodermic needle off the floor, but was still unsteady getting on her feet. I grabbed both of her arms and she slammed her forehead against my chin. I fell back and she grabbed my throat with both hands and squeezed as hard as she could. I brought both my arms up between hers and broke her grip. I wrapped the wire attached to my wrist around her neck and then unbuckled the wristband from my arm. Pulling it tight, I looped it into a secure knot. She pulled a plastic bag with white powder in it out of her bra, and attempted to put it in my face. I shoved her out the open door. She slammed against the outside of the plane as the wire broke her neck. I stood to the one side of the plane door and could see her lifeless body, still finely dressed, being slammed against the plane with hurricane force, dangling by her neck. I went and unattached the wire from the plane door hinge and then managed to close the door with a pull strap. That was quite an effort!

I brushed the white powder off my shoulders and chest, then I sat back down in my plane seat. Everyone started waking up.

"Sorry, sir, I seemed to have drifted off to sleep. Oh, I must have slept in a bad position, too. My neck hurts."

"That's okay, James. You must have been exhausted from our Tehran trip. I think we all are. Look, everyone else is napping too."

James stood up and looked. Sure enough everyone else was sound asleep.

"Well, then, I don't feel so badly about it, just so long as our pilot is still awake."

I went to the front and knocked on the pilot's door.

"Is everything okay in there, Arthur?"

The door opened, and Arthur said, "Yes, everything is fine. We are over the Aegean Sea at the present. Is everything okay back here? I did have a door ajar signal a little while ago, but it seems to have corrected itself."

"Everything seems to be fine, Arthur. All of our doors are secure. I checked them myself."

"Hmmn, well then, maybe I will have the plane mechanic look at the doors when we get to Geneva. You can never be too careful about these things. We don't need a door blowing open. Someone could get blown out. Where's the young lady? Powder room?"

"Yes, she decided to take a powder."

7.

Chapter Seven

Safe in Harm's Way

"Well, Sir, all of my information points to the NSC, and possibly its head, McFarlane, not the President. It could be someone under McFarlane, doing it without his knowledge. We are secretly sending missiles and other weapons to Iran in some sort of on-going deal not approved by Congress." I told Sir while on the phone as we approached Greece in my jet.

"Send me your documentation when you get on the ground, Zeb. We need to review it. Great job. I knew we could count on you. The President still isn't clear of suspicion. Treason is much deeper than that. There are other things going on, possible ties with not just China but Russia as well. There is some sort of smoke screen in the government hiding this information. You are a necessary and indispensable agent for us. Without you we would be practically blind to these things. The Council wants to keep you on payroll permanently. Does that sound agreeable to you?"

"Will I have the same privileges that I have now?"

"Absolutely. We know we can trust you to get the job done. Now, with that said, we need you to go to Beirut, Lebanon, ASAP. There is a report that there is a possible Islamist terrorist group that poses considerable danger there. We need to find out what is going on, and you are the man to find it out. You will meet with Alby Ameer at the

American University's Museum of Natural History. By the way, this Islamist group is connected to Iran, so we are not completely done investigating that situation. It is all connected."

"Athens International Airport in eight minutes..." came the voice of Arthur over the loud speaker.

"We will be looking forward to hearing from you soon." Sir hung up the phone.

We all buckled our safety belts and waited to touch down in Athens. It was a smooth landing and we soon were inside the airport terminal. They had many fine shops and eateries. I decided to stop at the first one we came to, where we took a few minutes to relax and satisfy our appetites. After that I found an Office Max store there where they faxed my reports to Sir for me. I wasn't quite sure of how secure that was by sending it that way, but I was assured by the store personal that the only copies possible were that which I retained and that of the destination. I had the fax sent encrypted, so I felt that I didn't need to find a government facility to do what I had to do. I wasn't sure I could trust a government facility, so maybe this was the best. Unlike the Tehran Airport, here we felt relatively safe.

We browsed around the airport while the plane was checked out and re-fueled. Everyone took turns going into the restroom and snack shops as we toured the airport. Arthur busied himself with plotting a flight plan, while I looked back over the documents that I had just sent. There were unnamed operators in the financial pipelines. Destinations were deleted in a few cases. Three of the files were CIA files marked Top Secret. I didn't understand what they were doing in Iran, unless someone sold the weapons directly to the Iranian Central Bank. Those three documents were signed at the bottom by "Loveit." I wasn't sure if that was a man's name or some sort of code word. It could have just been an expression of appreciation, "Love it!" Anything was possible.

"The Dasher Plane is now ready for boarding!" came an announcement over the airport loudspeaker.

"Well, that was pretty quick," I told James. "Arthur is getting better." We all walked toward the exit gate that led to where our jet was waiting. Suddenly, I heard something zing past my left ear. I thought it was a bug at first until another one flew past my right ear.

"Get down!" Burt yelled. I was being shot at! I fell flat to the concrete while my two bodyguards scrambled to handle the problem.

"It looks like someone has put a price on your head," Chet yelled as he pulled out his .45 pistol. Suddenly, the attackers disappeared.

"Where did they go?" I called out, still lying on the floor.

"I don't know. I guess they didn't want to tangle, just assassinate," Burt said as he put his gun away.

"Be careful, they could be cloaked and you wouldn't see them," I warned.

"Cloaked? You mean like invisible?" Chet asked as he put away his gun.

"Invisible, yes, I've never seen it before I came to Geneva. It is a new secret technology." I said.

"American?" Burt inquired.

"Chinese," I replied.

"That is a game changer," Burt said.

I've only seen one cloaking blanket, but apparently there are more," I informed them. "I actually have one."

"Don't you think we will be safer in the plane, and in the air than here?" James asked.

"You are right, James. Let's go!" I said, and we all hurried to the plane that was waiting for us to take off. We all piled in and got into our seats as quickly as we could. Once strapped in, we taxied down the run way, and were shortly in the air headed for the dangers that waited for us in Beirut.

"ETA for Beirut is in two hours..." Arthur announced over the loud speaker.

After we reached cruising altitude, James got out of his seat, and served us drinks and refreshments. I didn't think to get a waitress for the flight. I guess I was too busy dodging bullets to do that. James did a fine job of taking care of us, but a waitress would have looked better in my opinion.

"This certainly is relaxing," I remarked to James as he made his rounds.

"Better enjoy it, Mr. Dasher. Beirut may be a trying experience. I'm concerned that it may be more dangerous than Tehran."

"It may be indeed worse. God will protect us, James. Besides, we have two excellent guards with us."

After an hour and a half of uneventful, relaxing flight, and while we were still over the Aegean Sea, suddenly I was startled by a loud explosion that came from the back of the plane. There became a strong current of wind through the plane. I looked back and could see that an explosion had taken out the back side door and part of the plane's fuselage.

"What happened?" I yelled.

"I think maybe someone at the airport planted a bomb on our plane!" Burt yelled over the rushing sound of the wind.

"Or Miss Ching," I said

I pulled my telephone down from the ceiling and called Arthur.

"Our back door has been blown out. Can we make it to the airport?" I asked.

"Negative. It seems like the back tail wing has been damaged. We are losing altitude. I can't get the plane to come up, We probably aren't going to make land. You better prepare for either a bail out or a crash landing. I think you would be better off bailing out, sir. The crash landing may not be very soft. There is no way to predict that sort of thing. There are parachutes above everyone's seat."

"If we bail out, you need to bail out also, Arthur."

"Negative, a captain goes down with his ship, sir. I'm going to take this thing as far as it can stay up. I recommend bailing out soon while we still have good altitude."

"Alright, everyone, parachutes are above your heads. Get them on, we are bailing out!" I yelled. I strapped my suitcase to my pants belt so that I didn't have to hold on to it. It was supposed to be waterproof, but I had never tested that feature of it.

Everyone scrambled and got their chutes on. Chet and Burt who were military trained had no problem putting their chutes on, but James had quite a struggle with his. Burt finally had to help him with it after he got his own on properly. We all slowly maneuvered over to the front door. Burt said it was better to go out the front door because we would clear the back tail wing more easily. I didn't know much about parachute jumping even though I had done it before, but not under these circumstances. So, we took Burt's advice and opened the door. Once the front door was opened the plane seemed even more unstable. It must have made Arthur's job even more difficult.

"All right! On the count of three, we start jumping, one after another. We need to jump close together so we can stay together," Burt announced. He stood by the door. "After you jump, count to three and pull the cord that is in your hand. Got it? We need to do this now, soon we will be too low to jump! Right, James, you are first," Burt pushed him out the door. I watched James' parachute open. Burt grabbed my arm and pulled me to the door opening. "See you down below," he said and shoved me out into the wind. I counted my three seconds and pulled the cord. It didn't open. I waited a second and pulled it again and nothing happened. Next, I pulled the reserve parachute. The canopy came out but was tangled. In order to keep from having a free fall into the water, I was able to pull the reserve canopy into a shape that helped slow me. I crashed into the water not far from the others. It knocked the wind out of me, but I didn't sustain serious injuries. Land could be seen at a considerable distance. The plane was still in the air and looked to be over land at the time.

"Are you okay?" James, being the first to come up to me, asked.

"Yes, I think so. Seems like not only was the plane sabotaged, but so was my parachute." That made me think that whoever sabotaged my chute knew where I was sitting. That would leave me to believe that a fellow crew member attempted to take my life, or again, Miss Ching. Immediately I thought it may be Chet since he came up with the idea that someone had placed a price on my head. The other suspect was my pilot, Arthur since he was with the plane most of the time. I thought him to be the most probable, besides Miss Ching, but time would tell.

"It looks like we are in for a long swim, Mr. Dasher. Are you up to it? You had quite a fall," Burt called out to me as he swam up.

"I think so. I'll do my best," I told him.

"I hate to tell you this, but this is shark infested waters," Chet said as he stopped in front of the group. "I just saw several of them over there," he went on to say as he pointed. I looked over where he pointed and could see for myself several dorsal fins.

"Well, right now, they aren't between us and the shore," I said.

"That's a good thing. Whatever you do, don't splash. We need to be as silent and slow moving as possible toward land. Keep your eye on them, They like to ambush their prey, so keep facing them as we go." Chet said. We all slowly pushed ourselves through the water in calm, easy strokes. It made the shore seem twice as far away, but at least we weren't being attacked.

Suddenly, I saw one swim by me.

"Use your suitcase to keep it off of you," Burt said. "Don't let it take a bite. That will be the end of you and probably all of us."

Again, the shark passed closely by. I unsnapped my suitcase from my belt and held it between me and the shark. On its third pass, it bumped the suitcase, and then moved on. It didn't return. We all breathlessly watched it swim away. The whole group of sharks soon disappeared as we became close to shore. Finally, we were able to come up on shore, safe at last, so we thought.

A man who was walking along the beach at some distance to us, stopped and watched us as we sat down in the sand. Unexpectantly, I heard a shot ring out. I looked up and the man had a hand gun. James expressed pain and then slumped over in the sand. The man took aim again, and fired. He shot at me and missed since I dropped to the ground. I heard another gun go off, a different gun. I looked up, and the shooter was lying motionless on the ground. Chet was standing holding his gun out. He was a better shot than the would be assassin.

"James, are you alive?" I asked. We all gathered around him.

"Yes, I think so. I am wounded in the left arm," he said.

Burt came over to him and inspected the wound. "It's just a flesh wound, not deep." He said. Chet went over to the dead man on the beach and pulled a cloth off the corpse. He brought it back and gave it to Burt. Burt used it to wrap James' wound.

"Okay, that was a close call, but you will be alright. Nothing to write home to mom about," Burt said.

"Yeah, but it really hurts!" James complained.

"Don't complain, you are alive aren't you?" Burt said. "I do know medical first aide if we need it."

"Well, now that there is a reward over my head, our situation becomes much more dangerous, men. Is there anyone of you who wants to quit and leave? You are free to go if you want," I said.

Everyone thought just for a moment, and then, all affirmed their steadfastness to our mission. I was rather surprised. I didn't think there were people this loyal in the world anymore, but there they were, all standing with me, except of course, Arthur. I began to wonder about Arthur. Did the plane make it, or did it crash somewhere on its way to the airport? Did Arthur sabotage the plane and my parachute? If we made it to the airport without being shot, we may find out the answer to those questions.

THE TWISTED CASE OF THE PRESIDENTIAL CONSPIRACY

"Hey, Mr. Dasher, what about that cloaking blanket that you said you had. How about using it?" James suggested. "If they don't see you, they won't shoot at us."

"You know James has a good point," Burt said.

"It may save our lives. Bullets can come from any direction in this country," Chet said.

"You are absolutely right. I have it here in my suitcase," I opened the suitcase up and pulled the mysterious blanket out from under some clothing. "It just may get a little hot under this thing, but we will still be alive." It was a remarkable thing. I could barely distinguish an outline to the blanket as I held it in my hands. It didn't seem to work too well with a complicated background, but with simple greens like lawns or walls it was really pretty good.

"What are you waiting on? The sooner you put that thing on, the safer we will be," James said.

I quickly threw the blanket around me, and adjusted it so that most of my head and face were covered. I had to be careful not to reveal my feet as I walked. This meant that I had to take shorter than normal steps. That was a disadvantage that slowed our walk, but it was a small price to pay for increased safety. We could see a paved road that ran parallel to the beach, so we decided to walk it. If we went to our left, it took us further inland to the city, which is where we wanted to go. The sign said, "Paris Avenue." I could see a lighthouse to the one side of the road. I decided to walk behind the rest of the group since some of them kept tramping on my feet and blanket, if I walked with them or in front of them. I tried to keep up best I could, but it was difficult since they couldn't easily see where I was some of the time.

"If I remember correctly, Paris Avenue will take us to the American University here in Beirut," I said. " I have been here before on different investigations."

"Great, just stay under that blanket, is all I ask," Burt said.

9.

Chapter Nine:

Questions with No Answers

When we got to the American University of Beirut, I took the cloak off, folded it up, and placed it back in my suitcase. I didn't remember where the Museum of Natural History was so we had to find it first. James located a map of the college which helped speed things along. Shortly, we walked into the museum and approached the front desk.

"Is there an Alby Ameer in the library?" I asked the elderly woman seated behind the desk.

"Alby Ameer is the head librarian. His office is to your left. His secretary's desk is by the door. You will need to stop there first," she said with a crackly voice and a frown.

We walked over to the head librarian's secretary desk and waited to be recognized. She was busy with her filing cabinet at first, then she turned to us.

"Yeeehaas...." She said. Everything about her was strange. She looked masculine, muscular, wore a blonde wig, and had a light mustache. Her shoes didn't seem to fit. Her arms were curly hairy. She had pink glasses that had sharp points of both sides. I stepped back away from the desk.

"We are here to see Alby Ameer," Burt said as he stepped up to the desk. She didn't seem to bother him.

"Dooo yooouh have an aah-pppointment?" Now, she began to slur and sputter her words.

"Just tell Alby Ameer that Mr. Zeb Dasher is here to see him," Burt said gruffly. He clearly didn't like her.

The secretary got up from the desk and went into the room behind her. She stayed there for several minutes before returning to her desk.

"Heeeh, will seeee yoouh now," she said and pointed to the door.

"Thank you very much," I said and we went into the office behind her designated, "Head Librarian." Inside, there were several lounge chairs, and four large chairs in front of a very large mahogany desk. There was no one else in the room.

The secretary poked her head in the door and said, "Alby Ameer will beee wit yooouh in a minut." Then, she slammed the door shut. It almost sounded like she locked the door, but I wasn't sure of that. We sat and waited in the chairs for twenty minutes and then a person in a business suit came in from a door to the right of the desk.

"Hello, I am Alby Ameer," the man said. He looked remarkably similar to the secretary. No blonde wig, just very short dark hair, and the mustache was the same. Curly haired dark arms, and the same height. I surmised that this was the same person as the secretary, only dressed as a man this time. "I have been expecting you, Mr. Dasher. I am rather surprised to see that you actually made it."

"Yes, I'm not surprised. We are here on a fact finding mission for the United States of America," I said. "Can you tell us of any terrorist movements in this local area?"

"Oh, you are straight forward in your questions. I like that. No beating around the bush, so to speak. Yes, well, I really know nothing. I'm afraid the terrorists don't consult with me. I am just a librarian."

"You know Mohammad Farzin though don't you? How about Abdul Abebe? You don't claim to know him I suppose." I said.

"Who are they?" he asked.

"I thought you would be more cooperative. You have assets in the states don't you?"

"Well, yes. I have a home in California, and one in the D.C. area. Why?"

"Because, those will be seized by the United States government if I don't get truthful answers!" I said loudly. It was a bluff, but I had to put pressure on this man somehow, or I would not get anything out of him. He knew something I was sure of it.

"You look an awfully lot like your secretary," Chet said.

"My sister..."

He began to squirm in his chair. "Sorry, but I know nothing, really. Now, if you will excuse me, I have things to attend to."

"You aren't going anywhere, yet," I said. "Burt, Chet we need to show this man how we get information from people who insist on the hard way." Both Chet and Bert stood up and went to Ameer's chair. They towered over him.

"I have no answers for you." He said looking up at them.

"You can do it the easy way or the hard way. It is up to you." I said as the two body guards roughly pulled him out of his chair.

"Okay, wait, wait. I'll tell you what you want to know, but it may cost me my life."

"Well, you can choose the living death that I offer you instead. These two men were asking me for just the chance to hurt you. I mean really badly. Do you have hospital insurance?"

"Okay, let go of me, and I'll tell you what you want to know," he said.

"All of it?"

"All of it."

Chet and Burt let go of the man's arms and legs and he sat back down in his chair.

"Alright, go ahead." I said, Chet and Burt remained standing beside his chair.

"Yes, I know Mohammad Fargin. I received a payment from him just yesterday. He is financing with American money laundered through Kiev, the Hamas terrorist group in the eastern part of the city. I act as his coordinator here. American agents receive kickbacks from the transactions"

"So, what are you coordinating?"

"Explosions, both foreign and domestic. I expedite the payments."

"So, the domestic includes local?" I asked. He just sat in his chair and didn't answer.

"Here in this city?"

I took that his silence was an affirmative answer, finally he said, "I have no answer to that question."

"Okay, what is the target?"

"What is the biggest target that you can think of?"

"This university?"

"I can not say."

"Is it military?"

"I have no answer."

"Mr. Ameer, stop playing games with me." Burt grabbed his arm but didn't do anything else.

"Okay. Yes, yes it is."

"When are these explosions supposed to happen?"

"Soon."

"Soon isn't good enough, Alby. Soon you won't have any teeth in your mouth. When are the explosions?"

"The day after tomorrow..."

"Do you have the names of the American's who are receiving kickbacks from Hamas?"

Suddenly the door that Albay Ameer had entered the room with, opened and a man with an automatic rifle stepped through the door. He opened fire right away and took out Mr. Ameer and then Burt.

Chet had enough time to kill the attacker with a single shot from his .45.

"We have to get out of here, now!" Chet shouted. We all jumped out of our chairs and rushed to the front door. It was indeed locked! "Out the side door!" Chet yelled. We all hurried to the door and stopped there. The door opened to an empty stairway. "Let's go! Chet said. "Burt is dead, leave him. There's nothing we can do about it." We ran down the stairway to a basement. There we found a door that opened out on the street.

"You may want to put your cloak on, Mr. Dasher," James said. "We will probably all be safer if you did."

I quickly took the cloak out of my suitcase and put it around me.

"Great, now let's get out of here." Chet said.

"Where to?" I asked.

"I don't know, how about the airport?" Chet suggested.

"Good idea. Maybe our plane is there. I'll have to get another one if it isn't."

"Hey, there are several Beirut Airport taxi's over there," James said, pointing across the street. "One of them can take us to the airport."

We went across the street and stopped at the driver's door on the first taxi that we came to.

"Three to go to the airport please," James told the driver.

"Three? Where's the third one?" the driver asked.

"Oh, give him a minute, he's coming." Chet said.

I stepped to the one side and took the cloak off. I stuffed it into my suitcase in a hurry.

"Here he is!" James said.

"Good, get in," the driver said. He quickly went through the streets of the city and pulled up to the airport front terminal in just a few minutes.

"That will be twenty five American dollars," he said and held out his hand. " I gave him a fifty dollar bill and told him to keep the change. We got out and hurried into the terminal.

"Let's check to see if my plane is here, first," I said. "I can call Sir on the plane. We'll be going to Kiev."

"I wouldn't get my hopes up if I were you," Chet said.

"We won't know unless we look," I said, and we made our way to the observation deck where we could see just about the entire airport layout.

"Do you see it?" I asked.

"No, not really." James said.

"That doesn't answer the question of what happened to it though does it?"

10.

Chapter Ten:

A Friendly Visit to Ukraine

"Over there, isn't that it?" I said pointing to a tail section sticking out of a hanger.

"I think it just may be your plane. The back tail section is damaged. Let's go and get a closer look," James said.

We left the observation deck and went to the hanger that housed the plane. James carried my suitcase.

"Mr. Dasher. Your plane has had significant damage done to its fuselage. It will take six months to repair it," a tech said as we looked the plane over.

"Six months? Where can I buy a new plane?"

"See the man in building two. He has some for sale. Check with him," the tech said.

We hurried over to building two, which stood next to the main terminal. It only had one office with serval others being closed and locked.

"Is there someone here who sells jet passenger planes?" I asked as soon as we walked through the front door.

"That would be me," a man sitting behind a desk toward the back of the room said. "What sort of plane are you looking for?"

"My plane is two doors down, you can see it from here. Do you have something similar?"

THE TWISTED CASE OF THE PRESIDENTIAL CONSPIRACY

"You may like the Gulfstream G500 I have at a reasonable price. It's a beautiful plane."

"Is it here?"

"Yes."

"I'll take it. Where do I sign? Insurance also."

The man quickly pulled paperwork out of a file, and set on the desk. He put large x's as to where I was to sign, while he added the total.

"How will you pay, sir. Who will you finance through? We have our own finance program if you don't have one."

"I pay in gold," I said and handed him my Royal Gold Omega Card. "The card itself is gold."

"Hmm, I thought these were black cards. Gold? Surely you jest! I've never seen a card quite like this. I'm afraid I can't take it. Do you have another way to pay?" He reached out and took the papers back.

"It doesn't matter what you've seen before, put this in your card machine and the card will pay the total bill. Just try it. It does have a chip and stripe."

"I need your full address, sir, and ID."

"Run the card!"

The man reluctantly put the card into the card reader, and waited a few seconds. Suddenly, it was done, and the machine printed out a receipt.

"What's this? Paid in full?" the man sputtered. "You just bought yourself a plane."

I handed him an ID and signed the paperwork for the plane.

"Done?"

"Well, yes, I guess so. You will find the plane just on the other side of Building Two. It's actually fueled and ready to fly, a little bonus that I do for all my customers."

"Now, all I need is a pilot," I said. "Do you know of any good, independent pilots?"

"I do, but all are busy at the moment."

"Great," we walked out of the office and found the new plane on the other side of Building Two. "Looks like a great plane, doesn't it?"

"Really nice!" Chet said in response.

We walked around the plane admiring it, when suddenly Arthur came around the corner from the neighboring hanger.

"Mr. Dasher, I'm afraid the plane isn't going to be ready to fly for quite some time. What are we going to do?"

I was surprised to see my pilot, "Arthur! We had no idea where you were. What we will do is fly this new one instead! We are already fueled up. I have business in Kiev."

"Ukraine?"

"Yes, you need to plot the flight plan ASAP, please. I want to leave."

James, Chet and I went inside the plane and looked it over. It was a very good selection and smelled new. We settled into the comfortable seating in the front executive section. Arthur got into the plane in a little while and climbed into his seat in the cockpit. Soon the nice, quiet jet engines were started and taking us down the run way. Once in the air, I was soon on the "gogo" phone talking to Sir.

"In two days a military target will be hit with an explosion set off by the Hamas terrorist group in Beirut. We need to put our troops on high alert, immediately," I said.

"Do you have any further details? That is rather vague, No documentation; no names?"

"That is all that I could get out of my informant before he was killed. We barely escaped with our lives from Beirut."

"Are you alright?" Sir asked.

"Yes, I have lost a body guard. Burt was killed along with my informant. Could you see to it that Burt's body is picked up at the museum, and taken back to his family for burial?"

"That's too bad. Sorry to hear about his death. Yes, we will take care of Burt for you. He was killed in the line of duty. You may hire more men if you feel like you need to do so. As you well know. I have given you full authority to act as needed."

"Thank you, and I deeply appreciate that. It certainly has helped."

"Of course, as always, that being said, you really are therefore acting alone, with no actual traceable ties to the U.S. government, whatsoever. We will disavowal any knowledge of you or your operation. Your credentials and finances are all international. Where are you now?"

"I'm in my new plane flying to Kiev."

"Kiev?"

"Yes, my informant told me that there was U.S. money laundering going through Kiev that eventually went to the terrorists and then back to American agents."

"We need names, and documents. All you can get. We are still analyzing what you sent from Tehran."

"I think that we may be looking at a Russian connection also, not just Chinese."

"That is correct. This whole affair is deeply global. Certain people are getting filthy rich at our expense, Zeb. Our country is being undermined from within."

"I will keep you updated, Sir."

"Thank you. I am looking forward to hearing from you next time with more solid information. Get documents!"

"Will do, Sir." I said and hung up the phone.

After two refuel stops in eastern Europe, we finally arrived in Kiev. It seemed like a long journey, probably because it was. I had been to Kiev before, and I had some of my own contacts, but I wasn't sure that they would be any good for my present investigation. I started out with my best known contact, Earnest West.

He was a former CIA agent, and had also worked in the Intelligence Department for a decade. He now was more or less what I would call a free-lance man. He told me that he made more money that way than working for the government. He may be helpful. I called him from our hotel room in down town Kiev.

"Zeb! Whoa, what a surprise. It is good to hear from you. What is going on? There must be something important going down for you to call."

"We need to talk in private. I'm here in Kiev. Meet me in the lobby of the Opera Hotel in an hour. Can you do that?"

"For you? Sure. I am presently working a couple cases, but I can powwow with you for old times' sake if nothing else. I'll be there in less than an hour."

I hung up the phone and jumped in the shower. I put on a nice suit that James had purchased for me in a nearby clothing store. Arthur, James and Burt had separate, but adjacent rooms at this hotel. They also bought new cloths in Kiev before we settled into our executive suites. After I was satisfied that I was ready, I hurried on down to the lobby. Chet followed, but not too closely. I took a seat near the front door and Chet sat on the opposite side of the room.

Earnest walked through the front door shortly and saw me immediately.

He shook my hand and sat down in a seat near me.

"Zeb! Great to see you. I heard that you were dead, but you know how that is. The Intelligence Department poops out plenty of garbage. It's best to ignore ninety percent of it and go with your own instincts."

"No argument there. So, how have you been Earnest? Staying busy?"

"I'd say, too busy."

"Good, then, you may be able to help me with my project."

"Sure, be glad to do so. What is it that I can help you with?"

"Money laundering. Do you know anything about how the U.S. is money laundering through Kiev? Some of it is going to Tehran, some to China, some to Russia, and some to certain people in D.C. are getting kickbacks They are spreading the wealth."

"I have heard, but nothing solid. I can probably come up with some names and places if you give me a little time. How about this same time tomorrow. What is your room number, I'll call you."

"I believe it is room 501, Earnest."

"Zeb, this will require money. Some of my informants require payment for information. Do you have cash?"

I reached into my pocket and counted out five thousand dollars, "Will this due for starts?"

"Maybe for starts. Good, reliable information isn't cheap, and hard to come by."

"Just let me know what you need Earnest. Call me." I said and went back up to my room on the fifth floor.

Ten O'clock that night I received a call from Earnest.

"Belgorod, Russia. Adrian Oskesh." Earnest whispered once, and then his phone went dead.

11.

Chapter Eleven:

Struggle in Russia

"We buy a car and drive to the border," I said. "After that, I go in alone. James you and Arthur will stay here at the hotel. Chet will come with me to the border and drop me off. Chet will then return here to the hotel and wait for a notification from me. If you don't hear from me with in ten days, pack up and go back to Geneva. Here is the number to Sir. Let him know what has happened. From the Russian border I will find a way in, I am taking my cloak with me."

"Great, when do we leave?"

"The sooner the better as far as I'm concerned," I said, and then called the front desk. They got me in contact with a car dealership. Chet and I rode a taxi to the dealership where I picked out a common looking, used car. I didn't want anything that would draw attention to our travels because I intended to blend in the best I could. A poor man's car was perfect. After the transaction was complete, Chet drove me back to the Hotel where I picked up a few things that would fit in my pockets and in a plastic shopping bag. I loaded up on candy bars. I wanted to travel light. The cloak took up most of the room in the shopping bag, but that was fine since I viewed it as one of my most valuable assets. I sort of wished that I could visit Mr. Graft's Shop in Geneva again, but that was impossible.

On the way to the border, Chet said, "You know Belgorod is twenty five miles from the border don't you?"

"I knew it was a ways inside the border. Don't worry I'll find a way to get there. I will be fine. Just hang tight at the hotel, you will be hearing from me soon."

At the border, I got out of the car and wrapped the cloaking blanket around me the best I could.

"Good luck, sir," Chet said, and then drove off. I started walking until I came to where there were several houses grouped together. It wasn't large enough to be called a town or even a village. There, a flat bed truck was parked and running. I waited under a tree until I saw two men climb into the front, they looked to be heading in the direction that I was going, so I climbed up on the back of the truck and rode with them.

We were stopped by a Communist check point shortly down the road. One of the soldiers there walked around the truck, mostly looking under it. I could hear him speaking to the driver in Russian after that, and then he nodded to show that the truck was free to go. The road wasn't very smooth, so I had a rough ride the whole way. We finally came to a town, that I thought must be Belgorod. The truck stopped at a red brick building just inside the city limits. The two men got out and went inside. I climbed down from the truck, still in the cloak. Then, I saw a Russian soldier walking down the street towards me. Just at that moment, two young boys ran in front of me. They were picking up dirt and throwing it at each other, and laughing.

Suddenly I realized that some of the dirt flying through the air had landed on the cloak. I saw the Russian soldier stop in his tracks about thirty feet from me. He squinted his eyes, and then rubbed them. He was looking directly at me. I knew then for sure that I had become somewhat visible, probably semi-transparent from the dirt. The soldier lowered the sights of his rifle on me. I had to do something quick or this man was about to kill me.

I threw the cloak at him and ran. The soldier was confused at first, but then he threw the cloak down and shot. The bullet zipped past me on the right and I dodged behind the brick building. There were trees on the other side of the building, so I ran for cover there. I ran deep into the forest without looking back. When I finally did stop to look back I realized that there was no one chasing me. I was totally out of breath, so I sat down on a tree stump and rested. Then, I heard a twig snap behind me. I turned and there was a man standing there dressed in a suit.

"Shh, be quiet. There are men combing the woods looking for you, Mr. Dasher. Stay still here and you will be fine," he said in a hushed voice.

Immediately, I thought that this man was an American operative, and a person who could help me find my contact.

"Who are you?" I whispered.

"I am Dr. Francis Markus, research scientist."

"A research scientist in the Russian woods? What are you doing here?"

"I am here to help you complete this part of your mission. You are doing an important thing, you know, but you are somewhat unprepared for this leg of your journey. You will fail without my help."

"So, you are a CIA man?"

"Let's just say I do intelligence work."

"That's what I thought. So how are you going to help me?"

I'm going to lead you to your contact as soon as these pesky soldiers give up."

"So, then, Mr. doctor, who is my contact?"

"You were told Adrian Oskesh, but this is incorrect information given to thwart your mission. Your friend Earnest West had a gun to his head when he told you the wrong name. He is now dead."

"How do you know that? Were you there? That would make you a double agent!" I said and stood up.

"Shh, get back down unless you want to be seen. I was not there, but I still saw it happen."

"Hmmn, the CIA has cameras everywhere, even in Russia." I said and sat back down.

"Just a few minutes more, and they will start to clear out of here," Dr. Markus said.

"Who then, is my contact?" I asked.

"Vladimir Kercinko, he is from the Kremlin. He is a dangerous man, but in this case, he is the only one with the needed information who is willing to hand it over to an American agent."

"And why is he willing to betray his country?"

"He is not getting a cut of the money going through the pipeline. He feels left out, cheated, so he wants to destroy the operation."

"It's all about money then, isn't it?"

"Sadly, the worst part is the fact that there are politicians, who are willing to betray their fellow countryman for the sake of getting rich. They have been doing it for years."

Dr. Markus stopped talking and looked around. "They are gone now, Come on, we will go this direction. It will lead us out of the woods and directly to where Vladimir Kercinko is temporarily staying. I stood up and followed him. After about a half an hour of struggling through the woods and bushes we came to a small hut with a thatched roof.

"This is it. Just go in the front door. Vladimir is there sitting at a table waiting for you. He will have to leave soon to go back to the Kremlin so as to not arouse suspicion. The Kremlin has its own watchdogs that hover over its own people." Dr. Markus said. "Here, take this with you. Keep it until you need it," He handed me a small box and then pointed to the front door of the hut.

"Is this a weapon?"

"Oh no. What is in the box will help you out of a jam if you get into one. Okay? Don't lose it!"

"Sure. Thanks, I think."

"He's waiting."

I went to the front door and paused. I was hesitant to go in, unsure about what I would find on the other side of the door. I turned around to look at Dr. Markus and ask him if he was going to wait for me, but he was gone already. I didn't see him anywhere, so I figured that he had disappeared back into the woods. I turned the door knob and went in. There at a table I saw a man sitting with a glass of wine in his hand.

"Vladimir Kercinko?" I asked.

"Yes, who is asking?"

"Zeb Dasher."

"Good, I've been expecting you. This has to be brief. I must go soon."

"Do you have documents?"

"Yes, I do. I hope this will be sufficient. There's more, but it is stored in a highly secure vault. What I am giving you should tell you what you need." He handed me a thick file folder. I opened it and there were many documents of transactions and shipping invoices from the United States to Ukraine, with instructions on the covert path to Iran and even China.

"You mean Russia is coordinating transactions that go through Ukraine, then to Iran? It goes from Iran to China?"

"The documents are plain. There are those in the U.S who are making fortunes. I must go." The Russian spoke in perfect English. He got up and went out the back door. I sat there for a moment looking through the thick folder. It was devastating. It was not up to me to pass judgment, however. My job was to gather the needed information and hand it over to Sir. What happened to it from there was none of my business.

I gathered the paperwork back into the folder and got up from the table to leave when the door flew open. Six men rushed into the door and attempted to grab me. I struggled and broke free. Clinging to my documents I ran out the door followed closely by my attackers. I crashed through the woods with one of the men just steps behind me. I paused when I came to a deep embankment, and he flung himself on me. We both rolled down the hill to the bottom. There I got to my feet first, and picked up a large stick. The Russian struggled to his feet only for me to bash him on the side of the head. He fell limply to the ground. I looked up and saw the other five soldiers at the top of the hill. I knew I had to act fast. I struggled to get up the other side of the ravine as they rushed down the hill. I managed to get out of the ravine before they reached the bottom and I ran as hard as I could through the woods. The woods opened to a clearing that had a highway passing through it. I made my way down the highway as quickly as I could. A car pulled up beside me, and the driver motioned for me to get in. Without question, I jumped in the front passenger seat. I don't know who this was and he obviously didn't speak a word of English, but I appreciated the ride away from my pursuers.

I had no idea where we were going, but he kept driving. Little did I realize where we were going until we came to the outskirts of Moscow. I could see the Kremlin in the distance.

"Whoa! Let me out, please!" I said to the driver. I reached over and put my hand on the inside car door to let him know I needed out. He smiled and kept going. "Stop!" I demanded, but he accelerated instead. Now I knew I had a problem. We flew into the downtown area, and he stopped at what looked like the nearest police station. I attempted to open the door, but it was locked. The car had a window crank so I cranked the window down. I reached out to the exterior door handle and opened the door. I jumped out of the car and hurried down the street. I must have stuck out like a sore thumb because it seemed like every eye was on me. I looked back and the driver was out of the car talking to a man in a uniform. Then, I knew I was being turned into the authorities. I looked over at a car that had pulled up to stop at an intersection. Then, I made a desperate move and pulled the driver out of the driver's seat. I hoped in and turned the car around. I intended to go back the way I came.

12.

Chapter Twelve

My Russian Welcome:

THERE WERE NOW LIGHTS flashing behind me. I had about a city block head start on the city police car. It didn't seem like the car I was now driving had much power. Its ability to accelerate was definitely subpar but it was all I had. It did maneuver pretty well, and I managed to weave in and out of Moscow traffic pretty well. It was down one street and up the next, sometimes going the wrong direction in one way traffic. It was quite maddening. I could hear sirens going off all over Moscow. One would have thought World War III had started.

I saw a couple start to get out of their car just ahead. I quickly pulled up behind them and grabbed the keys out of the young man's hand. I took off in their car with the passenger door still ajar. It didn't matter. Now I had a different car, so I slowed down to avoid detection. I drove by screaming police cars going in the opposite direction. I figured that they would be soon setting up road blocks out of the city once they realized that they had lost me. I kept driving west, which shortly took me out of the city. I was on a pretty good sized highway, and felt relieved the further from Moscow that I got.

A police car pulled out behind me from a side road, and began following me. I sped up and he sped up. I knew then, it would only be moments before I would be stopped. Again, I decided to outmaneuver him. The car I was now driving was no better than the previous one. Pushing down on the accelerator didn't seem to do much at all except increase the sound of the motor. The speedometer read forty-five. I pulled on to small dirt road. It was a rough ride! The police car behind me was now right on my back bumper but he had not turned on his siren or lights. The dirt road sent up a cloud of dust and dirt into the police car. The car I was driving rattled severely as we crashed our way along the rough road. Suddenly, the engine stopped running. I pulled to a quick stop and jumped out of the car. There was an open field before me. I didn't know if I would be shot for running away, so I stood beside the car with my hands raised in the air and waited. The police car pulled up beside me and an officer got out of the car.

He was a large man with a frown. He walked over to me and spoke to me in Russian.

"I don't speak Russian. I speak English."

He said something else and acted disgusted. He spun me around and put handcuffs on me. I was placed in the back of the police car and he drove back to the police station in Moscow. There, he got me out of the car and took me into the station. I sat in a small, locked room for quite a while before someone in a suit came in. The door locked behind him.

"So, what are you doing in Moscow?" the man asked in rough English.

"I was seeing the sights. You have a beautiful city."

"So what are you doing with these documents I have here?" he asked sitting the thick folder that Vladimir Kercinko had given me on the table in front of me.

"Oh, those, those are part of my business. I am an American who was sent here to sort of check on the transaction process. We need to know from you if everything is going well or not. Are there adjustments needed?"

"So who sent you?"

"A Congressional Committee. They are the ones who are really running this operation.".

"So, who is your supervisor? Someone I can call to confirm this?"

"I can't give you that. I am not under any circumstances to reveal to anyone that information, as a matter of fact, I don't know his name."

"Well if that is the case, you will be transferred to a detention center in Siberia until we can either confirm your story or you give us the needed information. Right now, you will be held under the charge of espionage. You may be executed later on, but we will see."

The man left the room, leaving the folder on the desk in front of me. I reached over and grabbed the folder. I wanted to hang on to the folder if I could, but I was sure they would strip it away from me. I sat there in the chair for a good while before anyone came back to the door.

The door opened,

"Alright, take him out of here and load him in the van with the others. He can keep his file and whatever he has on him. It won't do him any good where he's going." The man said, as two armed soldiers came in and roughly pulled me out of my chair. Down the hall I was dragged by the arms and out the door to a waiting van. I was pulled into the van and cuffed to one of the seats. The sliding door slammed shut and the driver put the vehicle in gear. There were eight prisoners in the van including me, as well as one driver and one guard who sat in the front passenger seat. Two of the prisoners were young women, one person looked like a business man, the rest looked like commoners. The guard kept barking orders to the prisoners in Russian. I didn't have any idea of what he was saying, so I kept my eyes lowered and head down.

The van took us to a train station where we were loaded with other prisoners in box cars. There were no places to sit inside the car, and it got colder the closer the train came to Siberia. I didn't have any winter clothes on, so I became concerned about my survivability. The wood floor of the box car was very uncomfortable to sit on after a short while.

Lying down didn't help either. Many prisoners tried to stand and lean against the walls for as long as they could. Some leaned against each other. All looked forlorn. The prisoners in the box car looked like poor people, judging from their clothing, mostly elderly. The deeper into Siberia we went I realized the more difficult it would be to escape.

After many hours, we came to a stop and the train doors were opened, and we got out. We went to a long, wood framed building but were not permitted to go inside out of the cold. It was below freezing and there was snow on the ground. We were permitted to step inside the front entrance long enough to get a quick drink out of the water fountain there. Along the side of the wood framed building there was a row of out-houses that everyone had to use. The line was long, and everyone had to hurry because the train was to leave soon. They took about an hour to do something to the train engine, before we were loaded back in to the same box cars. Some of the people were not able to get drinks or use the bathroom because the time ran out.

More hours of enduring the swaying and rattling of the train going down the endless tracks. I lost track of time. We made several stops before coming to our final destination in tall snow country. We got off the train and were herded into long buildings that held rows of beds. Each person picked out their own bed. There was no place to put personal items or clothing. The camp had no outside security fencing since the snow and horrible weather insured that everyone stayed within the camp. There was no place to escape to since we were miles from any town.

I stopped in front of an empty bed. The single cover was tattered and well-worn around the edges. There was no pillow or sheets, just a dirty mattress. I looked over at the next bed and it looked to be in the same condition as the one I had stopped in front of. There was no need to shop for the best bed, they were all in terrible condition. There was one old pot-bellied stove in front of the long room. It would be our only source of heat. My bed was about a hundred feet away from it, so I would have to sleep in my clothing to stay warm.

It was dark when we had arrived. Someone in a uniform yelled something in Russian, and turned out the lights shortly after I picked out my bed. I put my file folder under the cover, and the little box that the strange man named Dr. Markus had given me. It was cold in the room, so I looked over at the pot-bellied stove, and there wasn't even a fire burning in it. The room would have to be warmed strictly by body heat. I pulled back the blanket and several roaches scurried away out of sight. Reluctantly, I laid down in the bed and pulled the blanket up to my ears. My shoes remained on otherwise my toes would have frozen. I could see my breath in the air and I realized that it would get colder in the building as the night went on. There were several frozen over windows that let light into the sleeping area from the moon. That night was a full moon so there was quite a bit of light even though the electric lights were turned out.

I lay there shivering for several hours. I could hear some people snoring throughout the room. It was impossible for me to sleep. I wasn't sure what was planned for tomorrow. I think we were going to be expected to do some sort of manual labor after sunrise. The front door opened and a guard came in and looked around, then he went back out, and closed the door behind him. My mind wandered after that until I thought of the little box that the stranger had given me. I hadn't even opened it yet. I remembered his words, "What is in the box will help you out of a jam." Now my curiosity was aroused. I sat up in the bed and put the file in my lap and then, I laid the little box on top of the file. I carefully removed the lid to the box. Inside, I saw a black, electronic cube with one small button on the top. I took the cube out of the box and found a note attached to it. It read, "Think of where you want to go and press the button. It works one time only!" So, this thing would read my mind or something? I put the cube and note in the box and put the lid back on it. Cute joke! So who was this Dr. Markus any ways?

Why would he try to prank me when he knew he wouldn't be around to see it?

The whole thing sort of upset me, so I pulled the cover back up to my ears and laid back down. Where would I want to go most? Any place but here, I thought. But, the answer had to be one place, and clear in my mind, perhaps for the Markus Magic Box to work! Right? I thought I was getting delusional just to even think about it. Maybe the box would flash a picture of where I wanted to go. That may be encouraging, perhaps or maybe depressing. It would be entertaining to press the button to see what the note meant, if anything. Why bother? It wouldn't hurt a thing if I did press that button. I would do it, and then lay back down, that way I wouldn't be thinking about it.

I sat up again, and once again laid the folder in my lap, and put the box on top of it. I carefully took the lid off and pulled the cube out. I turned it over several times and inspected it. It was two inches on each side. It had no features except for the one single button on its one side. I decided to go ahead with it, and concentrated on where I would like to be instead of this icebox. Geneva, my room in Geneva would be perfect. As I sat there watching the mist of my breath rise to the ceiling, I earnestly desired to be back in my room in Geneva. I pressed the button.

13.

Chapter Thirteen

Bumming It

The room got pitch dark in haze, and I felt very dizzy. I attempted to get out of bed, and fell flat on the floor. I felt like I couldn't get up or even open my eyes. I lay there until my strength returned and then I got to my feet. I looked around and was shocked and amazed to see that I was in my hotel suite in Geneva! The thick file was lying on my bed, but the little black cube was gone. What magic had been performed! This was impossible. I stood there rubbing my eyes for a moment, and then figured that I had to be either dreaming or I had snapped under the pressure and was now quite out of my mind. Had I been brought here, and just woke up? I walked around the bedroom and decided to call the desk.

"Front Desk, this is Mr. Twiggs, how may I help you?" It really was Twiggs! I was really in Geneva!

"Yes, this is Mr. Dasher. I am hungry, please send up some food, like roast chicken, mashed potatoes, and corn on the cob. I need it ASAP

"Mr. Dasher? When did you come in? I totally missed you."

"Tell Mr. Fried that I want my food in a hurry or I'm pulling out of here."

"Sir, yes sir. He will be glad to hear that you are back. Yes, yes, your food will be right away, sir." Mr. Twiggs said and hung up the service phone. While I waited for the doorbell to ring I quickly took a shower. The shower was very necessary, and I felt somewhat refreshed afterwards. I took one of my suits out of the closet and I was combing my hair when the food arrived at the front door. It was just what I had ordered. The cook at the hotel was superb. Even though I hadn't ordered anything extravagant, he made everything taste above and beyond the norm. I quickly devoured the food, and then sat down in an easy chair beside the bed. Next I decided to call my team who were still in Ukraine and get them back with me in Geneva.

I called the hotel where they still were. James answered the phone.

"James, this is Mr. Dasher. I am in Geneva. I need you all here, now. Get on the plane and get here ASAP."

"Oh, Mr. Dasher. It is good to hear your voice again. We were worried about you. Since you haven't contacted us, we were preparing to go back to Geneva today, as you had instructed us to do."

"Great, is everyone okay?" I asked.

"Everyone is okay. I'll tell them that you called, and we'll be there as soon as Arthur can get us there."

"Is there something wrong with the plane?"

"No, not at all. We will be leaving soon, then."

"Thank you. Just come up to the suite when you get here. I'll be waiting for you." I said and hung up the phone. After that, I called Sir and told him that I was sending the Ukraine documents to him. He was appreciative of my success. I took my documents down to the hotel desk and had them crypto-fax each sheet to Sir. I had a few leads that I wanted to follow to tidy up the investigation, but I would have to wait until my crew got back to Geneva. In the meantime I decided to relax and lounge around the hotel and the city.

I only took two hundred dollars out of my envelope and put it in my vest pocket. I left all my important things in the suite safe before leaving. Downstairs I looked in the restaurant area, and decided that I wasn't hungry enough to order anything yet after eating that chicken meal earlier. So, I walked out of the front door of the hotel and leisurely strolled down the street. I looked in the windows of many different business, and then I remembered Graf's Shop. I wondered if he had gotten anything new in that I might find interesting. The other items that he had sold me proved to be very helpful. I decided to go there. As I walked down the street, I could tell someone began walking very closely behind me. Suddenly, I felt the barrel of a handgun in my ribs.

"Down this street here, Turn..." came a rough voice from behind me. "Don't turn around. Keep going."

I made a turn down the street that I was directed to go down, and then I was shoved into a small space between two buildings. It wasn't even the size of an alley but proved to be a walkway designed to be a shortcut between blocks.

"Stop!" came the voice, and then I felt a heavy blow to the back of my head. I woke up later with a severe pain in my head and neck. I had been robbed. They took my jacket, money and even my shoes. I had been roughed up considerably while unconscious. My nice white shirt was dirty and torn. I struggled to my feet and made my way out of the walkway. I slowly was making my way back towards the hotel when a police car pulled up next to the curb and stopped. A policeman got out of the car and started speaking to me in French. I had a bad headache and didn't feel like listening to gibberish, so I started walking again. The policeman didn't take kindly to being ignored, so he came around in front of me and stopped.

"What do you want?" I asked.

"You are American?"

I said, "Yes,"

"Let me see your ID and passport," he demanded.

"I don't have any of that. I was just robbed. I stay at the Woodward Hotel not far from here. All my ID and passports are in the hotel safe."

I looked over at a man standing nearby. He looked at me and snickered.

"What's so funny? Have you never seen someone who has been robbed before?" I said in exasperation.

"No, I'm afraid not, since I have just been robbed, also, and you are the one who robbed me."

"What?" I recognized the voice. This was the man who had just robbed me! "I recognize your voice. Officer this is the man who robbed me!"

"You can positively identify him? You saw his face?"

"No, but I know the voice!" I explained.

"Sir, this man is a bum, and he forced me into the byway and took my money."

"You positively identify him, sir?" the officer asked my robber.

"Positively,"

"And how much money did he take?"

"Two hundred dollars."

"Wait a minute, officer, that is what he took from me. Look, he robbed me, see I don't have the money on me! He has it. Make him show you his pockets!" I pulled my pockets out so that they displayed the fact that there was nothing in them. "He needs to empty his pockets. That will show who is telling the truth!"

"I have two hundred dollars, yes I do, but it is mine, not his. I kept it from him," the thief claimed.

"Let me see the money," the officer demanded.

The would be thief pulled the money out of his pants pocket and showed it to the officer.

"Look, we are almost to the Woodward, can we just walk down there? They will vouch for me. I rent an entire floor there. I can show you my ID and passport when we get there." I said, beginning to feel desperate.

"He's just trying to worm his way out of what he did, officer."

"It is only a little ways. What do you have to lose, officer? I want to demonstrate to you that I am not a bum and an thief. I have evidence of who I am. I don't need to rob anyone. I have money."

"Where did you get this money?"

"I work for the U.S. government. I am very well compensated for what I do."

"What do you do?" the officer asked.

"I do high level security. Right now I am doing an investigation in foreign exchanges."

"Okay, then, let's just take that walk to the hotel. Come on, both of you." The officer motioned for us to both start walking. He walked several steps behind us as we went. We walked into the hotel lobby and was greeted by Mr. Twiggs at the desk.

"Mr. Dasher! Sir! What has happened to you? Are you hurt?"

"Twiggs, tell the officer who I am, please."

Mr. Twiggs looked at the officer and said in a sincere voice, "Oh, sir, you must excuse Mr. Dasher, he is normally well dressed. He is one of our VIP guests of royalty here, and highly respected. Is he accused of something? I can assure you, he is a person of the highest character."

"Royalty? That answers that," the officer said and turned to the robber. Hand the two hundred dollars over to this man."

The robber slowly pulled the money back out of his pocket and handed it back to me. As soon as I had it in my hand, he bolted away from us, and ran out the door.

"Excuse me…" the officer said and ran after the man.

"Thank you, Twiggs. I have to go up to my suite now." I said and turned to go to the elevator when I saw a familiar Chinese face. It was Miss Ching. She was standing near the elevator door, as if she were waiting for me. The thought came into my mind that she was somehow connected to the robbery. I made my way over to the elevator.

"Well, Miss Ching. What brings you my way?

"Oh, family matters, that's all. Not to worry. It doesn't involve your international business enterprises. Oh, dear, what has happened to you? Are you hurt?"

"I had a little scuffle down the street. I must go get cleaned up," I said as the elevator door opened for me.

"If you would like to have dinner with me, I'll be in the lobby at 7:00 this evening." She said.

"Oh sure. That is great. It gives me time to clean up first. I'll see you then." I said and went up to my room thinking about the possible reasons Miss Ching was here and so friendly. My crew should arrive shortly, so I probably had an interesting rest of day ahead of me.

14.

Chapter Fourteen

An Evening Out

At five p.m. James and the rest of the crew walked through my front door. I was sure glad to see them. It seemed like months!

"You are a sight for sore eyes, my friends!" I said.

"We're just checking in with you to notify you that we are here safe and sound," Chet said.

"I'm going to my room. If anything let me know," James said.

"The plane is fine, This new one is better than the old one. We need to hang on to it." Arthur said standing in the doorway.

"Hopefully, we will." I replied. Everyone went to their rooms to shower and relax.

I got myself ready for my evening meal and meeting with Miss Ching. I debated about telling her that her sister was dead, and that I pushed her out of my plane's door. It was a matter of self-defense, but she may not see it that way. I decided not to speak about such things that may upset her, unless of course, it was unavoidable. It was seven o'clock more quickly than I realized since I was almost asleep on the sofa by that time. I hurried down to the lobby and found Miss Ching sitting on one of the hotel sofa's with a stranger.

I walked up to Miss Chang, "Sorry, I'm a bit late. I almost fell asleep. So, you never mentioned bringing a friend along."

Miss Ching and the stranger both stood up, "Oh, sorry about that. He's an old friend that I didn't know was staying here. I just happened to see him come in a few minutes ago. "

"Will you be joining us at the dinner table.... What did you say your name was?" I asked.

The stout looking man, mid-thirties, said, "Phil, Phil Dyrt. No, I can't join you this time. I must be going. I just thought I'd say a word to Ching and then go up to my room." He wore his dark hair rather long and plastered flat on his head with some sort of greasy ointment. He had glasses that had large, round thick lenses.

"Dirt? As in fill dirt?"

"Dirt is spelled with a y not and I," he replied with a snort.

"But it's still dirt. My name is Zeb Dasher."

"The great Zeb Dasher? You are quite famous. Its an honor to meet you sir. Now, if you will excuse me, I must be going," he nervously said and turned to leave. He stumbled over an expensive floor pot that housed a rare flower that only blooms every twenty years. The hotel had been nurturing it for years. It had just finally reached the point of blooming until now. The flower and dirt spilled over the ornate carpet.

Picking himself up off the floor, he said, "Oh, they shouldn't have things like that out on the floor to trip people." Dyrt said, trampling clumsily on the exotic flower until it was flattened.

Twiggs came over and surveyed the mess on the floor.

"Sir, are you all right? We have an in house physician if you need one." Twiggs said. "Your suit is certainly dirty now, also. Shall we have it cleaned for you?"

"No, that won't be necessary. Thank you just the same," Mr. Dyrt said with a strange and inappropriate chuckle. He left us and went to the elevators. Twiggs examined the shattered pot. The plant was hopelessly crushed. Upset, Twiggs went back to the desk and notified the janitor crew that there was an emergency spill in the lobby.

"Oh, you must excuse Mr. Dyrt. He is such a klutz."

"Weird, very weird in my opinion, I'm afraid he killed their rare flower. That pot wasn't cheap either."

"Oh, I wouldn't doubt that. He has a talent for killing and destroying things."

"Where would you like to go to eat, my dear?" I asked.

"Oh by far, the Dans le Noir at the Ritz–Carlton. It is one of my favorite places to eat."

"If you like it, that's good enough for me," I said. "Twiggs, can we get a car for the evening, please."

"Yes, of course. I will have one at the front door for you momentarily, sir." He said as he picked up the desk phone.

We walked to the hotel's front door and paused.

"So, how do you know Mr. Dirt?"

"Oh, he has done things for me in the past. I've known him for years. He is awkward, but gets the job done."

"What does he do?"

"Oh, he is my clean-up man, more or less."

"Some clean-up man. I'm impressed." I looked back at the clean up crew trying to get the soil stains out of the beautiful carpet.

Ching smiled, "You haven't seen him in action. He is a quite proficient."

"I'm sure he would be."

Oh, you will be impressed."

I saw a black limousine pull up to the front door. The chuffer got out and opened the doors.

"That's us, dear," I said. We got into the car and was taken to the Ritz-Carlton. Miss Ching seemed to know her way around there, and knew all the waiters. We were ushered over to a fine, private table and sat down.

"What do you think you would like?" I asked after we got settled and handed a menu. It was in French. "Oh," I said, "Would you order for both of us, please. I don't know much of the French language, so I better not try to order."

Ching smiled, "Oh, that would be just fine with me. I know just what is really good here. Whatever we order will be superb.'

"Great, if you will excuse me, I must go to the men's room. Be a dear and order for me if the waiter comes while I'm gone, please."

"Ching smiled and replied, "Oh that would not be a problem, Hurry back."

I got up from the table and found my way to the men's room. It had a large walk-in lounge area just inside the door, and then a place where they shined customer's shoes for them. There was an array of phones by the door, so I stopped and called my suite back at the hotel. James answered.

"Hello James, this is Mr. Dasher. I need you to research a Phil Dirt for me. Dirt is spelled with a y instead of an i. Please let me know as soon as you can give me some info in him. Call me back at the Ritz-Carlton restaurant called the Dans le Noir. Thanks. I need it in a hurry."

"We're on it sir," James replied and hung up.

I went back to the table and the food and drinks were already there. I sat down opposite Ching.

"Wow, this looks fabulous!" I said.

"It tastes even better!" Ching said with a smile.

Neither one of us said much as we ate, and I was full once I was through the three courses.

"More dessert?" she asked.

"Oh, no, I am just fine," I replied with a friendly smile.

I heard an announcement called over a speaker that had my name to it.

"You have a phone call, Zeb. They will bring a phone to the table." Miss Ching said. We waited a moment and a waiter brought a phone to the table and plugged it into a phone socket mounted under the table.

"Zeb here," I said. It was James.

"This Dirt guy, he is listed by the IDF in Israel as a suspected assassin, nothing solid there. Just a suspect. MI5 also has him as a possible anarchist conspirator wanted for questioning in several bombings and assassinations in the U.K. but no solid convictions or arrests. He is wanted by Scotland Yard as a larceny suspect. That is it. He seems to have been spotted on photographs at all of these events, but nothing solid. No convictions."

"So this goofy guy is dangerous? I think he looks to be more dangerous to himself than anyone else. His looks are deceptive, " I said and hung up the phone.

"Well, it appears your Mr. Dirt has some dirt on his background,"
I said as they took the phone away.

"Oh really, Zeb. I don't know him all that well. I've just had dealing with him a couple of times, that is all," she said with a smile.

She reached across the table and took both of my hands in hers. "Can't we just enjoy each other's company for the night and not be concerned about other things?"

I looked in her beautiful eyes. She looked so gorgeous, and enticing. This was a dangerous woman.

"I suppose we could look at it that way just for the evening."
I replied.

"Great, now let's finish here and go to my place. Shall we?" She raised her hand and the waiter quickly brought over the billing check. I took it and paid for the meal and drinks. It totaled $678.49 in U.S. dollars. I left a two hundred dollar tip. I brought thousand dollars with me, since I left my Omega Card in the hotel safe, so I had enough to take care of my anticipated expenses. We went out front and they brought the car around. Our chuffer kindly opened and shut the doors for us. Miss Ching told the driver the address, and we left the restaurant.

"Did you enjoy your meal, Zeb?"

"Oh yes, it was a fine meal. Everything was perfect. You certainly know your restaurants." I said and relaxed back into the plush limousine seat.

"Thank you, I like to think that I do. My hotel room is just as fine. My bed is in the shape of a heart, Zeb, all in pink. Do you like that idea."

"Well, it sounds nice enough. Is it comfortable? That's what counts as far as beds are concerned."

"Oh yes, especially with you beside me, it will be especially comfy tonight."

She leaned over and kissed me on the lips.

"You have my attention, trust me," I said.

Soon the limousine pulled up to the hotel and we got out. Ching spoke to the desk clerk as we walked to the elevator.

"I'm on the sixth floor," She said as she pressed the floor button.

Her room was like an apartment, very nicely decorated. She poured me a drink and excused herself to change into something more comfortable.

I sat down in a large easy chair and sipped a little of my drink as I waited for her to come out of her bedroom. In a short while she came out in a skimpy, red nighty.

"Wow, that looks nice! Kind of took my breath away,"

She came over to my chair and climbed onto my lap, facing me.

"Oh, I plan on taking your breath away back in the bedroom, so hold out until then. I'm going to do something special just for you. It will be fun," she said with a big smile

She started to undress me starting with my tie, then my sports jacket, and then my shirt. She sat and admired my muscular stature.

"Come on, back here, hurry now." She said pulling me by my hand. "While I'm in the mood."

"Okay then," I said and quickly got out of the chair. I followed her to her dimly lit bedroom where I found that she did have a heart shaped bed. There, she pushed me from behind and I fell into the bed.

"Here, have a drink. I am thirsty tonight," she said while handing me a half full glass and poring herself one.

I took a small sip of it while she went over to the corner of the room and put on some soft music.

"Care for a snack before we get started, Zeb? I'm going to the kitchen to get something for myself. How about some chips or peanuts? I have chocolates, also. So, what will it be? Anything?"

I thought for a moment, and replied, "No, not right now. Maybe later I'll have something. I'm still full from the meal."

"Okay, I'll be right back. The television clicker is on the night stand. If you want to turn that on while I'm getting something to snack on, that will be okay. Pick out something romantic..." she said and left the room.

I wasn't interested in either television or music, so I just made myself comfortable on the bed. On the night stand on the other side of the bed, I found several, folded, typed papers. The name Loveit was signed at the bottom of each page. Evidence pointed to the fact that Loveit was an important name for Ching. I stuck the paperwork in my back pants pocket and waited for Ching.

In a few minutes, I felt dizzy and weak. It was then that I realized that the drink had been spiked with something. It was a good thing that I had only taken small sips of it. Ching took a long time in the kitchen, and I couldn't keep my eyes open long enough to see her come back in. I fell asleep briefly, but woke up when I heard Ching talking to someone.

"See, there he is. All knocked out. That wasn't so hard, now was it?" she said.

"No, not at all. He isn't as smart as they claim."

I recognized the voice. It was Phil Dirt! I opened my one eye slightly and could see them kissing! Now, that was a surprise.

THE TWISTED CASE OF THE PRESIDENTIAL CONSPIRACY

"I'll take his arms and drag him down to the car. It's waiting in the side street."

"You are taking him down the elevator?"

"No, I'll take him down the stairs. No one uses the stairs. I'd be seen in the elevator dragging him."

"Just wondering." She replied. "That's a lot of flights of stairs to take him down."

"It's easier to go down than up. I can push him down the steps, and he'll roll. So it won't be too bad. It might be bad for him, but not for me." Dirt said with his customary strange laugh at the end of each sentence.

I played dead and let him drag me to the front door of the apartment. He was already tired by that time and huffing and puffing. Ching opened the door and he gave me one final large push out the door. I landed with a thud on the hall floor.

"Wow! He weighs more than I thought! I'm already tired."

"Here, let me help you. You take the other arm. Let's go to the emergency stairway," Ching said. They both grabbed my arms and dragged me to the steel door and swung it open. Once the door was opened, they gave me one large push down the steps. I flew down the steps and stopped at the landing, thirteen steps below. I felt like I had been beaten on with a steel club. By that time I was fully awake and could move again. I stood up and prepared myself as they came down the stairs after me. They both stopped when they saw that I was ready for them. Phil chuckled and then jumped at me, while Ching ran back up the stairs.

I simply side stepped and Mr. Dirt flew past me and landed with a thud. He then crashed down the next flight of stairs. He lay motionless, sprawled out on the landing floor. I ran back up the steps to take care of the monster named Miss Ching. I found that she had locked herself in her apartment. By this time I figured that she had called the hotel security on me, so I left by the way of the stairs. On the way down, I saw

Mr. Dirt struggling to get to his feet, but he only clumsily fell down the next flight of steps. He was out again when I stepped over him. Once outside the hotel, I called James and had him pick me up.

On the way back, we were followed by a car. One time at a stop light, the back of our car was rammed, but no one got out of the car behind us. We certainly weren't getting out. Once we pulled into the hotel guest receiving area at the front door, the car drove on by.

Back in my hotel suite, I looked at the paperwork that bore the name Loveit. Several were congressional documents, two came from the office of the President, and one was from the Department of Defense. They were all approved by Loveit. I knew he couldn't be in each branch of government, so the only thing I could think of was that he was some sort of behind the scenes bureaucrat head. The civil service has" top brass that seem to weld great power. Loveit may be one of them. I had never heard of him, and I didn't know where he was in the American bureaucracy. It was dawning on me that America had a shadow government that ran things to profit themselves. The public and elected officials were expendables.

I got on the phone with Sir, and informed him that I was going to crypto-fax my Loveit documents. He sounded deeply interested in what I was saying. He had never heard of Loveit either. After I hung up the phone with him, I wondered if Loveit was a real name. It could be a name of an organization, a group, committee or a made up person. After I went down to the front desk and had my documents sent, I went back up to my suite and did a little research of my own. I kept my originals in the safe. My crew gathered around me and waited.

I made several calls to some friends in Congress, and none of them knew of a person named Loveit. I called my friend Rick Hasselton in Pennsylvania who on occasion had been helpful to me.

"Rick,"

"Zeb, are you done with your investigation? I'm surprised! I didn't think I would hear from you for quite some time."

"Surprised I'm still alive, more like. No, I don't think I am even close to being done with it. It seems to be quite a tangled mess. I need some information, Rick. Can I rely on you?"

Zeb! I'm shocked! Of course you can rely on me. I am you're long time friend, remember? It's just that sometimes things work the wrong way, and I can't fight it. I have to survive to help my friends like you. If I didn't look like I was cooperating with the higher ups, I would be eliminated. You wouldn't want that would you?"

"No, Rick. Now what I need is inside information on someone called Loveit. I think he, she or it works in the civil service as one of the higher-ups, possibly at the very top. I have documents with the name Loveit signed at the bottom that approves some big ticket items. Can you find out who this is, and any information that you can come up with regarding him?"

"Yes, I'll see what I can come up with. Loveit? No, I don't know of anyone in government with that name. So, this is not some wild goose chase that you are sending me on. This person actually exists?"

"No, I wouldn't waste your time with a wild goose chase. Loveit may be a group, committee or even a made up person for all I know. But, someone is signing official government papers by that name."

"This paper work is from what branch or branches of the government, you know like the Justice Department, the Senate, the DOD, what?" he asked.

"They are from many different branches of the government, Congress, the Department of Defense, even the White House."

"You have White House documents? What we are dealing with are high levels of security. When you said White House, you went to the top."

"So, see if you can find anything out for me."

"Okay, Zeb. I know you are working on something important, for the benefit of the people of America, so yes, I'll do what I can.

"Thank you Rick. I knew I could count on you, really. I'm staying at the Woodward Hotel in Geneva, Switzerland. Just call the desk and talk to Twiggs. He will pipe you up to my room."

"Geneva?"

"Yes, Geneva. I will be here probably for quite some time. I'll be waiting to hear from you, Rick. Thank you, Good-bye."

I hung up the phone and took a break. I relaxed for a while on the sofa, before the phone rang. It was Sir.

15.

Chapter Fifteen

Our Adventure in Bagdad

"We need you in Iran as soon as possible. We have intel that informs us that Abdul Abebe of the Iranian Army is ready to turn in secret received documents himself. This would be a complete surprise if this happened. He is an important man. We need you to bring him here to the United States for interrogation along with the documents. He will be waiting for you at the Al Hayat Hotel in Khorramshahr, Iran. This should be the frosting on the cake as far as your investigation goes. It may wrap things up if we can get enough information out of Abdul Abebe, otherwise you may have to go to China as perhaps a last leg in your journey. You may have to go there anyway if Abdul doesn't give us what we want. We have a man in China that we want also, but he may not be needed depending on Abdul."

"Iran? I barely made it out alive the last time I went there, Sir. Are you sure this is necessary? We have other leads. What about Loveit? Has anyone found anything on him?"

"Loveit? Sorry, can't help you on Loveit. Just get the job done..." Sir hung the phone up before I could say anything else. He obviously didn't want to talk about Loveit. It made me think that maybe Loveit was the key to the whole thing. I called Rick.

"Rick, have you found out anything about Loveit?"

"No, not yet. You sure are in a hurry about him, aren't you?"

THE TWISTED CASE OF THE PRESIDENTIAL CONSPIRACY

"No one else is apparently. Now, I have to go to Iran and then maybe even Communist China. It seems like the Committee wants me dead or something by sending me on missions that are impossible to live through."

"Sounds rough Zeb, but you are the legend. You do the impossible."

"Why because I'm not dead yet?"

"What do you want me to say? I don't have any information on Loveit, yet, do you want me to make something up and feed you a lie? Come on. High clearance information takes time. It's like prying a fish out of an alligator's jaws by hand, but I'm doing what I can. I will let you know. Now be a good boy and go to Iran."

I hung the phone up. I had James purchase another pen camera from Graf's that would fit in my shirt pocket. It looked like and worked like a pen, but if I pushed the clip half way around, it would take continuous pictures. I was glad to get it when James finally handed it to me. I immediately put it in my pocket and kept it there until I needed it. I came up with an alternate plan that may help keep me alive. I asked Chet if he knew of men I could hire of military background who would be willing to go to Iraq. He got on the phone and called several times to various people.

"How many do you want, boss?" he asked while holding the phone up to his ear.

One hundred and armed with the best equipment," I replied.

Chet told whoever he was talking to what I wanted then hung up the phone.

"You got it. This won't be cheap. They want half up front, and the other half once they come back."

"Done," I said.

"They are sending someone up to the suite for payment."

"You trust these people?" I asked.

"With my life," he replied.

"James, I need you to go to Iraq and pretend that you are me. We are going to fly you and these soldiers to the Saddam International Airport in Bagdad. You will stay in Bagdad using my ID. This will make the powers that be think that I'm staying in Bagdad. I won't be there. Instead, Chet and I will be flown by Arthur to the border of Iran and be dropped off there. From there we will sneak our way into Iran, find Abdul Abebe, and bring him across the border where Arthur will be waiting. The hundred soldiers are for a show of presence. James, Saddam will think that you are a visiting military investor and welcome you. Just play the part, James. It is a diversion."

"We will need hazard pay," James stated.

"Not a problem," I said. The front door bell rang. James opened the door and a tough looking military man stepped inside.

"I'm Max from the Mercenary Militia Organization. I'm here for payment."

James ushered him over to me. I was waiting in the middle of the front room.

"I pay by card, " I said..

"Fine, most don't use cash. I have a processor here." He pulled a white, flat box with a keyboard on it out of his briefcase. He walked over to the wall and plugged the box into the phone outlet. "Card please," He said and held out his hand. I gave him the card and he put it in the devise. "It's good, here's your card back. You will pay the rest upon completion of the mission. When do you need the men?" He handed the card back to me.

"Tomorrow," I said. "We will be leaving at ten in the morning. They need to meet me at the Heathrow Airport, Building B. James call Twiggs downstairs and have him find out what size of suit Saddam Hussein wears, and get one here first thing in the morning, preferably from Paris. We need first class clothing. You will give it to him as a gift. He isn't into jewelry. He likes fine clothing."

"We'll be there, See you in the morning, " Max said and then left.

"That means I need to line up another jet, preferably military. It must be one large enough to carry one hundred soldiers. James, you will need one of my ID's for the trip, so I'll make sure you get it before we leave. Arthur, get the airport on the phone. I need that plane. James, don't forget the suit for Saddam."

The next day came soon enough. We met at the airport as planned.

Arthur could only come up with an old used military transport plane to carry the soldiers. He hired an Arab pilot to take James and the crew to Bagdad. That was fine, no one had a complaint that they weren't riding in luxury. I gave James the billionaire military investor credentials out of my packet that had my name on them, and Fifty-five thousand dollars in cash. The flown-in suit for Saddam arrived just before we left the hotel, so we were all set.

We saw the plane off, heading directly to Bagdad. My private plane would take a more roundabout way to Iraq's eastern border. Once approaching its outer border we would fly low enough to avoid radar. It would be quiet a flight, but confidence was high. My only serious concern was our dealings with Abdul Abebe in Iran itself. There was nothing about all of that situation that wasn't extremely dangerous. The others wanted hazard pay just for sitting at the Bagdad airport. Saddam was a madman by most reports, but he would welcome someone with money who was a military investor. I wasn't worried about them, they had it made compared to my assignment.

Arthur figured out how to get into Iran by a round-about, but much longer way through Armenia. It was a rather unorthodox path, but it wouldn't be as subject to military scrutiny as if we had come in from the west. We fueled up in Turkey and then again in southern Armenia. This route put days on to our flight, but we eventually made Iran's eastern airspace. The low altitude flight would exhaust the fuel, so that we would barely make it back into Armenia. We would met up with Arthur back in Geneva.

"Our landing spot is just ahead, Zeb," Arthur said.

"It certainly was a long trip. I hope we know what we are doing." I said as I looked at the terrain down below.

"This is not a friendly country. We are just inside the Iran border, fixing to set down sir. Fasten your seat belt. I will taxi to a stop, let you out, and then take off again. I will wait for you to the west of here, out of the country. Fuel won't permit me to go far.

"Meet me here tomorrow at this same time. If I'm not here, consider me dead and get out of here. James will be leaving Bagdad tomorrow also." I said as Arthur closed the plane door. Now, I was on my own, facing who knows what, ahead of me. I would soon find out.

16.

Chapter Sixteen

A Captive in Iran

This was an area of mostly dry flat land, but the city was near a waterway. I had no real place to hide, so I started walking. I watched the plane take off and fly out of sight. I walked toward a city that I could see in the distance. It was Khorramshahr. I stopped on the shore of the waterway. There was a man in a small row boat near the shore who saw me. I motioned him to come to me, which he did. I didn't speak his language so I gave him a gold coin and indicated I wanted to get to the other side so I could enter the city. He gladly accepted the gold coin and took me across the water. There, I thanked the man the best I could and he paddled away.

I walked into the city and found a city map posted on a billboard that showed the location of the hotel. There it was, the Al Hayat Hotel. How could I ever forget that name?! It wasn't very far away, so I picked up my pace. I was anxious to get there and find Abdul. The streets were busy, and I sort of blended in with other people on the sidewalk. I found that most of the people of the city dressed no different than people of the west. Several times people passed by me speaking English. Then, I saw it close-up, the actual hotel. It was large and reminded me of a temple.

The lobby was large and modern. I looked around and saw a man sitting in a chair at the other side of the room. I approached him.

"Abdul? It is Abdul isn't it?"

He looked up, "Yes, it is, and you are Zeb Dasher. We met once before, remember? Under different circumstances, of course, you might say."

"Yes, you have your documents?"

"I have them, yes," he said and stood up. "They are in the manager's office. Come with me and I'll give them to you."

We walked past the front lobby desk and he opened the door to an office. Walking in he said, "Of course I have everything that you want, but it comes with a price you know. Everything has a price." He closed the door behind us.

"From what I understand there was no price in the agreement. You were to hand over the documents and surrender to me."

"Surrender to you?" Abdul chuckled. "I never said that to anyone. They have it all backwards, must be the translator the general uses. I originally said that you come to get the documents and in exchange, you surrender to me. That was the price to be paid for the documents, your freedom. So, no one will receive the documents since you didn't bring anyone with you to take them out of here, so I guess I'll keep them." He smiled.

"I'm afraid you are going to have a problem collecting your fee, Abdul." I said.

"Well, I have a collection agency to do that for me," he said and opened the door. In rushed six men who attacked me. I am expert in the martial arts, and I overcame them all in just a few minutes. Abdul was a little frightened when the last man dropped, so he called for help.

"Well, you know the same will happen to those you call, so yes, you are going to surrender to me, Abdul," I said as I approached him. Two more men rushed through the door. I knocked the first one down and wrestled the second one. While we struggled, the first man hit me from behind with a hard object and I was out.

"When I woke up, I was tied to a metal chair and in a dark room. I didn't know how long I had been unconscious. There was a bright light hanging over my head. It was so dark in the room, I couldn't tell how many people were there. I was not alone, since I could hear people moving around and breathing. Suddenly, I was slapped across the face.

"Ah, Mr. Dasher. We have been anxious to meet with you. You know a lot about the United States, do you not?" came a voice in the darkness.

"No, not really. They are the ones I'm investigating at the present time."

"So, you have learned much in your investigation, then?"

"No, not yet. I'm still working on it. You've caught me at a bad time, I'm still in the fact gathering stage."

"Well, then, we know that you know certain things. We could use this information to our advantage."

"You probably know more than I do. I should be asking the questions Why do you think I'm investigating them? I'm trying to learn some details."

"Details of what Mr. Dasher?"

"Dealings, military and monetary dealings."

"Right. And what of these military dealings?"

"I am looking at the money trail that goes through Ukraine , then here and trickling to China."

"Really, then."

"I really can't help you, even if you beat me to a pulp, I have nothing. Abdul was supposed to give me my needed information."

"Right, and he didn't did he?"

"No."

"Who sent you?"

"I have no names."

"I don't believe you Mr. Dasher..." suddenly I was slapped so hard that I went over, chair and all, to the floor. Two men set me back upright.

THE TWISTED CASE OF THE PRESIDENTIAL CONSPIRACY

"All right, Mr. Dasher," came the voice in darkness. "Back in D. C, you visited a select group of men on a secret committee. Who makes up that committee? Their names, Mr. Dasher. Their names!"

"Like I said, I don't know any names. They didn't give me any names. .." I was interrupted by another slap. "Okay, the only name I know is Mr. X. There, happy?"

"Mr. X? Well, thank you , Mr. Dasher. We've heard of Mr. X before from one of your predecessors who is now dead, Mr. Dasher. What is Mr. X's real name, Mr. Dasher?"

"Nobody in the committee has real names. That is how they keep it secret." I said with a bloody mouth.

"Really, now, Mr. Dasher, your level of cooperation is disappointing." Suddenly I was punched in the stomach. "Now, let that be a warning of worse things to come. Who was your contact in London?"

I realized that the stomach punch caused a violent involuntary reaction in my arms. I had actually snapped the ropes loose that secured me to the chair. No one realized it yet but me. I doubled over as if in pain and looked at the ropes around my ankles. It looked like I could slip the ropes off the bottoms of the legs of the chair if I could lift it up. I would have to be standing first.

"So, going back to Mr. X, then, where is he now? Is he in London also? We know you went to London, Mr. Dasher."

"You are so smart!" I said and suddenly stood up and punched my interrogator's face. The room was dark so I had missed and had scored only a glancing blow. I threw off the chair, and rushed into the darkness at my unseen captors. The only light in the room above me broke and I found myself fighting many men in the darkness. None of them were a match for my martial arts skills and physical strength. Soon, they were all on the floor, knocked out. I found the door handle and opened the door. The open door illuminated the dark interrogation room and I saw the man Abdul Abebe. I wasn't leaving without him. I reached down and snatched him up off the floor. He wasn't in very good condition, but he would have to do.

"Walk!" I said and pushed him out the door. He slowly stumbled away from me. I picked up his paperwork off his desk that he had left there, then I shoved him again toward another door. This was a door that opened to the streets.

"Really, do you think that you can take me out of this city?"

"I don't think so, I know so. Now get going if you know what is good for you. Anything funny and I will kill you with my bare hands. Do you understand that Abdul?"

"Yes."

"Remember, Bozo, I don't need a gun to kill you. One blow and you are done. Now get going." I again shoved him. We walked down the street and back the way I came. Mr. Abebe looked pretty shabby going down the street. He obviously had a broken nose and a black eye. Some blood was running out of his mouth, but no matter, he kept on going. We finally made it to the waterway and same little fishing boat was there. I motioned for him to come and pick us up, and he hurried over to us. I gave him two gold coins for me and my fellow traveler. He gladly took us to the other side. Once there, I wished him happiness and I gave him another coin.

Abebe and I walked back to the place the plane had dropped me off. I wasn't sure, but I thought that I had arrived in Iran yesterday, thinking that I may have been unconscious for a day. The plane wasn't there, so we waited. The day drew on, and still no plane.

"What are you keeping me out here in this desert for? We will die of thirst! We have no water. Let's go back to the city so we can get something to drink and eat," Abebe said.

"Nothing doing. We are staying right here. My plane will be here soon." It was almost sundown when I saw a plane coming in from the west, flying low. It had to be Arthur. It was Arthur! "There it is now!" I announced. Abdul didn't seem too pleased.

"It's a long ways to America," he said in a grumpy voice.

17.

Chapter Seventeen

China

After I personally handed Mr. Abdul Abebe and copies of his documents over to the Committee, to Mr. X's satisfaction, in New York City, I was instructed that I still needed to go into China to obtain the certainty of the final destinations of covert shipments of arms and computers. If someone was going to be accused of selling and shipping arms to China, it couldn't just be on paper. I needed photographic proof. Satellite photos were insufficient, so it had to be done in person. This could be far worse than even Iran was. I felt that things had worked out rather well for me in Iran. I was to go it alone into China so that my crew, except for Arthur, remained in New York. They were to wait there for further instruction from the Committee. I was pretty sure that this was a one way trip for me, and that I would never see freedom again, that is, if I lived. I bid them all a warm farewell when I left with Arthur in the jet, headed west. Mr. X gave me a thick envelop of instructions for this part of the investigation which I reviewed on my flight over the Pacific.

We did a one day lay-over in Hawaii and then off to yet another south western Pacific island or two. We did a series of leap-frog maneuvers through the islands until we finally landed in British Hong Kong. Arthur was to wait for me in Hong Kong. From there I was to find my own way behind the Communist border to the base at Sanya, China. Covert shipments from the U.S. were arriving there and going deep into China to a underground secret nuclear weapons plant being constructed named 816. It was in Chongqing. I picked up a good Chinese interpreter to take with me into China. He had formerly been with the U.S. military intelligence for over a decade, and was very familiar with south eastern China. His name was Kim Kim. I just called him Kim since his first name was the same as his last name. The info packet that I had received referred him to me. I independently hired him. I still had my Royal Gold Card, and I wasn't afraid to use it.

He put the word out to his contacts behind the Communist border that there was an American billionaire in town, who was interested in doing covert business with them in the field of military hardware, including nuclear assets. Super computers were also to be dangled in front of the Chinese as enticements. Perhaps it was just a dark web I wove on my way to the grave, I was alone, just Kim would be with me as my only help. I spoke no Chinese at all. I had no weapons either or even a definite plan of escape. No matter, I was hired to do a job, and it would be done, or in this case, die doing it.

We waited a few days on Hong Kong Island, during which I contemplated the seriousness of my situation. The third day, Kim came to my hotel room and told me that things were ready. He and I could leave under the cover of darkness that same night on a small boat that would ferry us across to a hidden dock on the main land. That was great, since I determined in myself that I would not worry about how things would turn out. Arthur wished me good luck when we left.

At one in the morning we met the small boat on the shore of the island. I gave the boatman his fee in Chinese currency as directed by Kim. The water was pretty choppy at that time causing the boat motor to struggle. From what I understood Kim to be saying in rough English was that there was a huge storm approaching from the ocean. We would be safe on the mainland by the time it arrived. Soon, we were on the other side, pulling up to an old run-down, dilapidated wooden dock that had half of its boards missing. It was well-hidden being recessed into a wild brush area of the shore. It looked as if it had not been used in years. Kim and I had to climb a steep bank, grabbing on to tree limbs and tall grass, to get up on solid dry ground from the dock.

"Well, Kim, we've made it this far. Now what?" I asked bluntly when we finally stood at the top of the hill.

"We run, Mr. Dasher. Over there at that house, we may hide." He pointed to a very small house that had just one door and no windows.

"Are you sure about that, Kim? That doesn't look like a place that I want to hide in."

"It is unused, and empty."

"People live in such tiny houses?"

"Yes, they live in what they can get."

"Okay, what other options do we have?"

"We keep moving, pressing on to our destination of Sanya. Do you prefer to do that tonight?"

"Yes, we need to keep moving. Is there any transportation available?"

"In the morning there will be. With your money, we can rent the transportation of your liking, Mr. Dasher. Right now, there is nothing."

"So, I see. Well, let's see how far we can get by morning. Oh, you must remember that my name here is J. Rothschild Hamilton."

"Yes, Mr. Hamilton." Kim didn't seem all that pleased, but he was hired to travel with me, so he had to put up with walking in the darkness. It was only a little after two when we started to walk. We walked until daybreak, which was after six-thirty. I estimated that we had walked over thirty miles by the time the sun came up good. Kim was shorter than me, and he had a problem keeping up with my long legs, so he was glad when we finally stopped and sat down off the road. People were early risers for the most part around there, so we began seeing people pass by. We got up and walked some more until an old rusty bus pulled up beside us and stopped. The bus door opened and the driver shouted something at us.

"He wants to know if we want a ride," Kim told me. I nodded my head, "yes," and the bus driver waved us on board. I handed the driver the fare, and we walked down its center isle.

The bus was old and the seats barely had any upholstery left on them remaining. There was just one other passenger on the bus, seated toward the front. Kim and I sat all the way in the back. The road was rough, and the shocks on the bus were obviously gone, so the bus rocked and squeaked as it made its way down the rough highway. We made several stops, got off one bus and on to another that was in just as bad of condition as the first. On we went, stopping here and there to pick someone else up or letting some lucky person off. I was glad when Kim said that we were coming into Sanya. It was a nice, well developed city, with modern buildings. Kim and I got off at the first stop just inside the city limits.

"Here, the show begins, Mr. Dasher. Once we get to the hotel, you will be treated like a visiting dignitary. You better dust yourself off, sir."

"Maybe, I could get some new, fresh clothes and shoes, there."

"Yes, I'm sure of it. A young man named Mr. Xi Jinping will met with you first. XI Jinping is the Deputy Secretary for the CCP in a northern province. He has come here just to see you. He is a rising political man, who may someday be the President. He wants to rise to the top, so he will be seriously interested in what you have to offer from the United States. They like doing business with the United States. You all seem so easy going, rich and helpful. I wonder sometimes if it isn't to your detriment."

"Great, Mr. Xi will be impressed with what I can offer him. It will be an unheard of offer."

"There is the hotel just ahead, sir. "

"Great, I'm ready to get this show started. If I can pull this off it will be a miracle."

THE TWISTED CASE OF THE PRESIDENTIAL CONSPIRACY

"Mr. Dasher is a legend even over here, sir."

"Yes, but here, at this time, I'm not Zeb Dasher, I'm the aristocrat, and military entrepreneur, J. Rothschild Hamilton."

"Yes, you are!" Kim said smilingly as we walked into the hotel lobby.

There we immediately saw that the lobby was full of Chinese military personnel, and several men dressed in business suits. We went to the hotel desk, where Kim spoke with the man behind the desk. The desk clerk pointed to several of the suited men sitting in a corner.

"That one there on the right is Xi. Come, he is waiting," Kim said.

"I do the talking. You do the translating," I said.

We walked over to the men seated in lobby chairs in the corner, and Kim spoke. The man on the right smiled and stood. He extended a hand out, and I shook it.

"I am J. Rothschild Hamilton. I am glad to meet you, sir," I said, and Kim repeated it in Chinese. He bowed in a traditional Chinese manner and I nodded my head in acknowledgement. He said something, and Kim repeated it back to me.

"I am Xi Jinping, and I am glad to meet you, sir. Welcome to the Peoples Republic of China. I hope you will find your stay here a pleasant one."

"Thank you sir, I'm sure I will. I have some business propositions for you to consider at your convenience."

"Of course, will you be staying here at this hotel, or another?"

"Probably this one, sir."

"There is a conference room over there, let's go ahead and talk," he said.

"Great, lead the way," I replied.

Kim and I walked with Xi along with two other men in suits, followed by a group of uniformed military men. We sat down at a table and said nothing for a moment.

"So, you have travelled all the way from the United States to do business with us, I am glad. What do you have to offer that we already are not getting?"

"What I am going to propose is that me and my associates supply you with advanced weaponry, and nuclear material at a greatly discounted price. We even have super computers on the table just for you."

"Super computers? What kind of nuclear material?"

"High grade uranium ore. We can get you uranium ore sent directly here instead of it going through other countries. It will be cheaper, faster and more convenient."

"How much ore are we talking about?"

"How much do you need?"

My answer brought a smile to Xi.

"Would you like to see our progress? With the help of our friends in America we are presently building the world's largest underground nuclear plant and weapons factory. It is out pride and joy. You may tour it for yourself so that you may be able to more accurately help us with our needs."

I looked over at Kim, and then back at Xi, "Yes, that would be great. I appreciate your helpfulness."

"Good then, Shall we go?"

"Oh yes, by all means," I replied with a smile. "I will need a compilation of recent past transactions and shipments, if you don't mind. This will be for our accounting department. It will help us with knowing your needs." I said. This would be perfect. I would get to see the construction of a secret military site as well as get shipping involves from Mr. Xi. He stopped and looked at me for a moment when I said that.

"We can do that for you Mr. Hamilton, if it will help."

"It will mainly help with our pricing."

"Oh, I see," he replied as we walked out to a waiting limousine. There were several of them lined up and ready to go. We got into the second limousine with Mr. Xi.

"I never get in the first car, for safety reasons, " he said as he sat back and relaxed. He looked over at me and smiled. I wasn't sure that I trusted the smile, but I smiled back.

"You never can be too careful." I said.

The entourage left Sanya and embarked on its journey to base 816 in Chongqing near Fuling. Xi made with a little small talk. He told me that his father had been an important man during Mao's reign while the Cultural Revolution took place back in the sixties. He had grown up with the elites and didn't mind trying to impress me with it. I attempted to sound interested and sympathetic, but wasn't sure that I came across as sincere being I was going through a translator. He continued to smile, so I assumed that he trusted me.

We arrived at a paved, arched entrance to a concrete underground facility that sat in a tall wooded mountain. It had one smoke stack sticking out of the top that looked rather odd and out of place. The whole thing was huge. The double doors slid open for us and we drove in and stopped. Xi got out of the limousine first, and waited for Kim and I to get out. I was impressed. As we walked Xi bragged about the advanced technology that was being developed at the facility. Construction on the underground military project had started back in the nineteen sixties. It still was not nearly finished. The nuclear reactors still were not present, and much of the equipment was only half completed, at best. As we toured the facility, and man came up and handed Xi a folder that contained the information that I had requested. He opened it, viewed its contents and then handed it to me.

"There, this is the information that you requested. Now, when you get back to your partners in the United States you will have prices and known needed items."

I took out my camera pen that James had gotten from Graf's store in Geneva, and pushed the clip halfway around. I clicked it and wrote a few notes on the pages Xi had just given to me. I then put the pen in my shirt pocket so that it could photograph everything as we toured the facility. I smiled and nodded at Xi, and thanked him for the information. The facility was quite large, and it took a while to finally complete the tour. A man came up to Xi and whispered something in his ear,. Xi shook my hand and told me that he had to go, He got into the second limousine and left. I got into the third limousine and was driven back to Sanya. There I got out of the limousine and walked into the hotel lobby as if I were going to check in, but only stayed long enough for the limos to drive off.

Kim and I then grabbed a bus going back to the place we got out of the boat. By that time the typhoon that we had heard about earlier was just coming ashore. The wind and rain was terrible. We went to the shore and the waves were huge so we went to the little house with only one door on it and stayed there until the storm passed by. During that time, it sounded like the little house was about to go with the wind, but amazingly, it stood through the storm. After the angry dark clouds rolled by, and things calmed down, we dared open the door and look out. There were trees lying in the streets, and some rooftops gone in surrounding houses. The streets were flooded with about an inch of water, but it was draining quickly. We went over to the shore looking for the man in the little boat, but saw nothing but choppy waves. It wasn't until the next day that we went back.

The boatman was nearby and he took us back to Hong Kong Island. I paid Kim a generous amount and thanked him. I met up with Arthur back at his hotel room and we flew out of there as soon as possible. Back in the states I turned in the invoices, and my photo pen to Mr. X. He told me that I needed to stay in New York for the day, and that he would contact me the next day. So I spent the night there in New York City and enjoyed myself. I was glad to be alive, because my trip to China could have been a whole lot worse. I found out later that the Chinese shut down the 816 shortly after I left. Apparently, it was no fun financing the secret project now that its existence was no longer a secret. The upper class in the communist party judged that it was too expensive to complete. I found out later that they made a tourist attraction out of it.

18.

Chapter Eighteen

The Taiwan Connection

X called me the next day and informed me that the person whom I inquired about to the committee, Loveit by name, was reported to be in Taiwan, just off the coast of China. Since Loveit had signed many of the documents of authorization, he was important to my investigation. Though I didn't cherish the thought of another long distant trip, I loaded my crew into my plane. I gave my plane a name. Every plane should have a name, so I named it White Lightning, since it was painted white, and it got me to places in a hurry.

It felt like I was spending more time in the air than on the ground. We basically followed the same path to Taiwan as we did Hong Kong.

After we landed in Taipei, Taiwan I had the definite feeling of "jet lag" when I got off the plane. I was just spending too much time flying, so I checked into a hotel and took the next day off. I went nowhere, but had room service bring my food to my room. I had a name, or part of one, but no picture, or where this person stayed. I had to find all that out for myself, since this person was invisible to the United States government. They could come up with no ID in any state of anyone that bore suspicion.

I began my investigation at the American Embassy otherwise known as the American Institute in Taiwan. They had no record of an American living or staying on the island with that name. I went to the city government's office building and looked at their records of passports, and found nothing. This person was obviously using an alias or was an imaginary figure used to either side track me, or confuse me. I leaned toward the theory that Loveit was only an imaginary person. The documents were perhaps signed by different people using that same name. The question was why would the committee think this person was real, or did they? Why would I be sent here in search of someone who may not exist?

Then, I decided to visit the high tech establishments on the island. The semi-conductor industry was still yet in its infancy stage of building, but would soon be an important industry on the island. So I decided to visit the small facility. There I was greeted at the desk by a Morris Chang. His name sounded familiar to me. I wondered if he was somehow related to Miss Ching. The names perhaps only similar.

"I am Zeb Dasher, Investigator for an American committee on military accountability."

'Yes, of course. I actually recognize you, Mr. Dasher. You are known even here in Taiwan."

He was friendly and then gave me a quick tour of his small facility. He had high hopes and expected his company to rapidly grow. Then, I asked him the question I wanted to ask all along,

"Mr. Chang, do you know of a Lovet either working here, or on the island? He deals with American purchasing. "

He thought for a moment, and then responded, "Yes, I have several orders from Loveit." He went over to a filing cabinet and pulled out a folder. "Here we go. Yes, he authorized the sizable acquisition of some chips that can be used for guided missiles several times. See, here." He handed the invoices to me. Several were signed, "I. Loveit."

"Very funny, Mr. Chang. I Loveit?"

"Yes, it is his real name. His first name is Isaac."

"Isaac?"

"Yes, he's associated with both the U.S. and Israel."

"Israel?"

"Some of these orders are funded by the United States, but go to Israel, also."

"Anything to Iran or China?"

"No, I don't believe so. No, just the U.S. and Israel."

"May I have copies of these documents for the Committee?"

"Certainly, I am glad to help with the United States in their follow-ups. There was a man from the CIA, I believe, who was here asking similar questions about acquisitions several weeks ago. He didn't mention Loveit."

"Really? Do you remember his name?"

"No, not really. It might have been Ron, Rick, or maybe even Randy. It began with an R. That's all I remember of him. I stay busy with other things that are more important. Sorry I can't help you with that." He said and then made copies of the invoices, statements and letters of request. He placed them in a folder and handed it to me. "Anything else that I can help you with?"

"This Isaac Loveit, does he stay on Taiwan Island?"

"No, from what I understand, he is a jet-setter. I don't know where he lives. Maybe, Israel. Maybe the U.S."

"Has he ever been here personally?"

"Yes." Mr. Chang said.

"Can you describe him for me?"

"I can do better than that. I have a picture of him."

"A picture of I Loveit? That is outstanding!"

"Yes, he was here with several other men, executives from other countries. My secretary snapped their picture while they were here. They wanted the picture, but she insisted that it was her camera and she had other pictures on the film. They left without it, I think it's still in her desk drawer." He said and we walked to the other side of the room to a small desk with a typewriter. A young lady was seated at the desk. Mr. Chang asked her about the photograph, and she looked through her drawers until she found it.

"Here it is, I thought I still had it," she said with a smile and handed it to Mr. Chang.

He looked at it briefly and then handed it to me.

"That's him in the middle."

"The man in the middle? He is a dead ringer for one of the six men that met me at the Hay-Adams Hotel in D.C. with Mr. X! He sat at the table with me and is part of the Committee."

"I wouldn't know about that Mr. Dasher."

"Well, it's possible that he just looks like the same man. I could be wrong."

"If he's part of the committee, it probably isn't the same man," Chang said.

"I hope not. I'm not sure what to think if that is the same man. Could you make a copy of this picture?"

"Certainly," Chang said and took the picture to the copy machine. He made a pretty good, color copy of the original, and handing it to me.

"Thank you sir. My nation thanks you." I said, shook his hand and left. I had perhaps gained valuable information with this one visit. I. Loveit just may be an Israeli agent, who went by various aliases to stay invisible. He was using tactics that I have used, so now, I am much wiser in whom I am dealing with. I met up with James and the crew at the hotel and we stayed until the following day. After that, I decided to head state side. We stopped over in Hawaii for fuel and a day's rest. The island is always a pleasant lay-over. The beach, the water and the people are all wonderful. Their food isn't bad either.

We left there and stopped in San Francisco. There are areas that are on the run-down side but for the most part, it is a beautiful city. I got us rooms at the Hilton Hotel, Union Square that seemed really nice. Then, I went in to the city's chief of police's office, Alex Coffman. He has been involved in several of my investigations. I solved an important case for him awhile back that gained him the chief of police job. He has

THE TWISTED CASE OF THE PRESIDENTIAL CONSPIRACY

always been helpful to me. His secretary knows me, and I just waved at her as I walked by her desk.

"He's in, but he's busy..." she said.

I knocked on his door and walked in without waiting for permission. He was seated at his desk with his head buried in paperwork.

He looked up. Seeing me put a big smile on his face.

"Zeb! I am glad to see you! Come in! I'm working on an important case, maybe you can help me with it."

"I'm kind of maxed out right now, Alex. What is it?"

"I'm afraid that I'm dealing with an international ring of thieves, Zeb. I've never seen the likes of them. They have just stolen one million dollars of the city's money here in San Francisco electronically. They hacked the First National Bank and just about wiped them out."

"That's a job for the FBI, Alex."

"Right, but they are dragging their feet. They should be on top of this case, but they really are just sitting on it.? There isn't even an investigation going on that I know of on their part."

"There could be a good reason for it, Alex."

"There may be a good reason for them to do nothing, but I have people pressuring me. They haven't even sent one agent over here. I just don't understand it."

"That is unusual. I'll tell you what, you get me all that you can on an Isaac Loveit, and I'll look into this bank job. Here is a picture of him."

"Great, I'll be happy to do that." He said with a smile. He went and made a copy of the picture and handed it back to me. "I'll run that through the photo ID program, and see what we come up with."

I left and went down to the First National Bank and went to the main-frame account link in the bank. They had a large computer complex that took up an entire room. I was able to access the master leger. After that I used a clone procedure of the new computer program that the FBI implements in one of these cases to back-track the withdrawal of funds from the bank. I've been involved in a few of their investigations of digital theft already. The technology was new, but it looked like it was the wave of the future. The new systems being implemented by the FBI and the banks were still somewhat experimental, and had a few kinks in them, but never the less, they proved to be helpful. Later, the same ideas became popularly known as the "internet." It showed the money went to Spain, then Ukraine, and then, Israel. It stopped there. I was surprised at the destination. Because the trail ended in Israel didn't necessarily mean that the money stayed in Israel.

I picked up the phone and called the chief of police. He was glad to get my call. I told him what I had found, and he overjoyed to get the information. I gave him the phone number to the bank that it was deposited in, and also the bank account number. He was shocked at how quickly I was able to obtain the information. He said that he may have something on Isaac Loveit by tomorrow. I went back to the hotel and we enjoyed a free evening in San Francisco.

19.

Chapter Nineteen

California Dreaming

In the morning, I went down to the hotel lobby and visited the snack bar. I took advantage of the fact that they had fresh donuts and cold drinks. James came down and joined me after a few minutes. I found a table to sit at and we both watched a little of the lobby television while we ate our donuts. Then, and strange looking man came over and sat at a table next to ours. He had a black derby hat and a black suit on with a long black beard and long curls in his hair that hung down just in front of his ears. I recognized him as being in Chasidic Jewish garb.

He looked over at me and said, "Hello, what brings you to San Francisco?"

"May I ask who you are, and why do you want to know?" I asked in return.

"Oh, I am sorry. I didn't mean to be offensive in any way. I was just being friendly. I'm Isaac Levit, and I live just north of here. I am here for a conference, how about you?"

"Nice to meet you Mr. Levit. I am Zeb Dasher, and I am here on federal government business. What kind of conference?"

"It is a Torah study by a most eminent rabbi that I attend each year."

"So, it's a big Bible study that brings you here."

"Bible? The Torah is the writings of Moses. God spoke to him, face to face."

"I see. Well, that is very nice. I hope that you get a lot out of your studies, Isaac."

"Thank You. May I buy you and your friend a drink?"

"Oh, no thank you. I appreciate the offer, but the free drinks here are just fine."

"I sense that you are a very thrifty man, Mr. Dasher. I worry not about cost, because I offer it in friendship. I would appreciate it if you accepted the drink as a token of your appreciation of that offer."

"Hmmn, it's not that I don't appreciate the gesture of appreciation, but I just don't need another drink." I replied with a smile.

"Oh, then, how about a nice warm strudel from the snack bar?"

"Well, that sounds good. I'll take an apple strudel." I said, but James declined the offer.

Isaac got up and went to the snack bar, and came back in just a few minutes carrying two hot strudels in napkins, one for him and one for me.

"Here, my new friend, enjoy." He said as he handed it to me.

He sat down again and bowed his head briefly as if to say a prayer, then he ate his strudel. My strudel was good and fresh. From what I understand, they made their breakfast items fresh each morning in the hotel bakery.

After we both finished our little breakfast snacks, Mr. Levit got up from his table.

"Thank you Mr. Dasher, for the pleasure of meeting you. You are quite famous you know. Now I must going. The meeting will soon start." He did a head nod and quick bow and then left. I sat there at the table and watched him go out the door. He looked back at me once before he left. He had a serious look on his face. I wondered about that.

"That man struck me as rather strange, did he to you?" I asked James.

"Yes, but there are a lot of strange people in this world, Mr. Dasher," he replied.

"Yes, you are right. Let's go up to the room and I'll call the chief. Maybe he's found something by now."

"I don't know; it's still early in the day. He may not be as fast as you are." James replied.

"Well, I'm done snacking, so we may as well go up anyway," I said and we went up to my room where the others were waiting.

"Any calls?" I asked Chet as we came through the door.

"None yet, sir."

"Well, that's okay, we probably will have to wait a day or two." I said and sat down on the sofa.

"You know that man we met down stairs at the lounge, his name was Isaac Levit. Isn't that awfully close to being the name of Isaac Loveit?" I asked James.

"Similar," he replied. "It could be just a co-incidence."

"Levit doesn't look like Loveit according to the picture I have." I said and pulled the picture out of my jacket pocket. The man in the picture is clean shaven with short hair...wait a minute, maybe I'm on to something, here. The man in the picture may not even be Loveit, but an impostor. Hmmn, The man down stairs, Levit may have been wearing a disguise. He was probably Loveit."

"So, you think that was him that we were just talking with?" James asked.

"There is a good possibility."

"So, why did he meet us?"

"He met us to give me an apple strudel, apparently."

"That doesn't sound good, boss," Chet said.

"Indeed not. He didn't plant anything on either one of us. He never touched either one of us."

"You ate it."

"The strudel? Yes, but that came from the bakery. Hmmn, well he did handle it. It's possible he put something undetectable in it for me to swallow."

"Maybe, a micro-transmitter." Chet suggested.

"Maybe, then I should induce vomiting, I need to do that in the bathroom just in case." I said and remained on the sofa. I attempted to get up, but my legs acted as if they had no strength. "Wait a minute, there is something wrong. I now can't move my legs!" I said in shock. Then my left arm started to feel numb. "Hey, it's spreading to my arms!"

"You have been poisoned!" Chet yelled.

"I'll call the house doctor! He needs to get up here right now!" James said as he grabbed the room phone.

"This may spread to your diaphragm and paralyze the muscles so you can't breathe," Chet said.

"It will stop my heart, Chet," I said, as I began to feel dizzy. The room began to swirl around me. My vision went dark. I could still hear Chet speaking to me, but I was unable to answer. It got difficult to breathe.

James rushed over to me and said, "The doctor is on his way up. Just hang in there, Mr. Dasher. The world needs you."

I woke up in the ICU at what was called Dignity Health of Central California. I had several IV lines hooked up and a monitor beside my bed. James, Chet and Arthur were all there in the room looking at me.

I couldn't get a clear view of them at first, but they seemed to be just floating. I felt like I was half dreaming.

"Hey, look, he's awake!" Arthur said, and he came near the bed.

"That's a definite improvement." Chet said with a smile.

A nurse came in and looked at the liquids that they were dripping into me through the IV's. Then, she checked my vital signs and noted them on her clipboard.

"He's coming around. That is a good sign. Mr. Dasher, can you hear me?"

"Yes," I whispered. "I can hear you, nurse. I must have been dreaming for days."

"You had a close call. We are glad that you are awake now. The police were here, yesterday, wanting to ask you questions, so they will probably show up today." The nurse said.

"Fine. I need to talk to chief Alex Coffman. James can you get him on the line for me?"

"Really, Mr. Dasher. You shouldn't be getting involved in business right now. You had a close call with death. You need to relax and regain your strength," she said. "The doctor will be in shortly."

James handed the phone to me after he got Chief Coffman on the line.

"Chief, Zeb Dasher here. Do you have anything for me?"

"There's not much on this man. He appears to be associated with the IDF. He has been reported as being sighted in Iran and China by American agents."

"Anything else?"

"Yes, he has visited the White House many times, as well as the Senate and the halls of Congress."

"So there ought to be plenty of information on him then. He has high clearance."

"No, it is as if who he met with and why he was there has been purged from the records."

"That's impossible," I said.

"Not really. I'm not lying to you. There basically isn't anything on this guy. The State Department says they have nothing on him," Chief Coffman said.

"If he has high clearance, there is a record of him somewhere. They just don't want to release the information. He must operate in the realm of top secrecy approved by the Administration. I think the San Francisco police may be looking for him since he tried to poison me."

"You? When did that happen? I was not aware of that."

"A couple of days ago, I think. I just woke up in the hospital."

"Okay, Zeb, maybe if we can find this guy, we will be able to get some information out of him."

"Thanks, Chief," I said and hung up the phone.

"Anything new?" James asked.

"Plenty. This case certainly gets more complicated as time goes on," I said.

The Chief posted an officer outside my hospital door for protection. I was to remain in the hospital for three more days before I was to be released.

20.

Chapter Twenty

Roaming in Rome

"We have video of this man, Isaac Loveit, at the airport, boarding a flight to Rome, Italy. And, Zeb, check this out, the million dollars that was stolen from our bank is no longer in Israel, but was transferred to Rome. Strange coincidence don't you think?" The chief told me onver the phone.

"This Isaac is into all sorts of high crimes, not just poisoning people, and swindling the American people, He's a big thief. " I replied. "Thanks for the information. I'll be on a plane to Rome today."

"Today? Aren't you in the hospital?"

"Yes, but I'm self-checking out even as we speak." I said as I climbed out of bed and disconnected all the IV's.

"Hey, before you go, I have a new account number in Israel that may help you to track the money down in Rome. Write it down."

I grabbed the paper off the nurses clipboard at the bottom of the bed and wrote the account number down. I folded the paper up and put it in my pocket. The drip monitor next to the bed began to sound an alarm. I went over to the room closet and found my clothes hanging there. I quickly put them on. Suddenly, I felt dizzy and had to steady myself.

"Mr. Dasher, you should not be doing this. You need to get back in bed," James said.

"I think we just experienced a strong earthquake, folks," Chet said.

"It wasn't just you, Zeb, but you still need to get back in bed," James insisted.

"Can't, we have important work to do. I can't be laying around sick. We are going to Rome and get the guy that did this to me."

"Rome?" Arthur said with a smile.

"Come on, let's get out of here before someone comes in," I said and we went out into the hall. There were several nurses down the hall at their station. The stairway was in the opposite direction, so we hurried down there. James had a rented car in the hospital parking deck. We wasted no time leaving. We went back to the hotel room that we had rented ever since we arrived in San Francisco and got our clothes, my folders and briefcase, and luggage. Next we hurried down to the airport and got in our plane. It was fueled and ready to go, so we took off as soon as we got clearance from the tower.

We fueled up again in New York City and then flew on to London and then, Rome. It was once again a lot of time in the air. I was thankful for having the plane and a good pilot. Shortly after we arrived in Rome and I obtained a large suite in at the four star Hotel Artemide. I made that my base of operations, as I have done in Geneva. I liked the place so well, that I decided to purchase the entire floor, and did the same to my penthouse suite in Geneva instead of permanently renting it. I needed permanent bases of operation, and purchasing them seemed to be a good investment. I put my all my files and valuables in the suite's large safe.

Next, I investigated where the million dollars from San Francisco landed. I was shocked to find out that the money landed in the IOR, or the Institute for the Works of Religion, otherwise known as the Vatican Bank. This was going to be a real problem, since the regulations for that bank were somewhat different than an American bank or even a regular bank in Italy. I needed someone to get me on the inside of the bank, not to rob it, but to investigate it. I had no way of knowing if Isaac Levit was still in Rome. I figured that the police department may be able to help with that. I chose to use my "Special Ambassador" ID credential and went to the police headquarters in downtown Rome. They supplied me with a translator. I showed the police chief the picture of Mr. Isaac Levit and he ran it through his "data base" which turned out to be a set of picture ID books and came up with nothing. His police department wasn't advanced as much as the one in San Francisco. I left there rather disappointedly. I decided to go and visit the nicer hotels in Rome and show them the picture of Isaac. I spent two days on that project, and came up with nothing. I figured that he either wore a disguise or this really wasn't a picture of Isaac. Though similar, he possibly wasn't the same man who tried to poison me. It seemed like all I was doing was roaming the streets looking for an invisible ghost who may no longer be there. Discouraged I took a day off from going anywhere, and just stayed in my room.

I decided to see what I could do at the Vatican. James called the Vatican Bank for me and made arrangements for me to speak to the bank president. It turned out that he spoke English and was initially educated at Stanford. This man was not only a banker, but he was an archbishop in the Roman Catholic Church. Archbishop Francis greeted me at his office door and welcomed me in. He wore a black Roman Catholic priest's garment with a reverse collar. He invited me to sit down.

"Tell me, Ambassador Dasher, what brings you from the United States to visit me?" he asked, and sat down behind his desk. I sat down in a nice chair on the other side of the desk.

I handed him the picture of my suspect, Levit.

"Have you ever seen or met this man?"

He looked at the picture steadfastly, and he shook his head, no.

"I'm sorry, but no. Is he someone of importance? Should I know him?"

"This man stole one million dollars from the Bank of San Francisco, and deposited here in your bank through an Israeli account."

"How did he do that? I would be aware of such a large transfer of funds."

"The money was wired here from Israel several days ago. He didn't cart it in physically."

"I see. A few days ago, you said? Here let me check the books. Do you have an account number?"

"Yes, and I have the account number from the bank in Tel-Aviv, Israel where it came from. Would that help?" I said and gave him the paper that I had in my pocket with the account numbers written on it. He looked at it and turned some pages in his bank ledger.

"No, this money has never been transferred here, Ambassador Dasher. There is no record of that large of an amount. It would be recorded here in this book. Sorry, the money has gone elsewhere." He closed the book and stood up. "Will you be staying in Rome long?" He raised his hand to shake mine. I stood up also.

"I don't know. I will probably stay until I find the man and the money."

"Sorry I was not able to help. How is everything in San Francisco after the quake?"

"Beautiful," I said. I didn't mention the strong earthquake that leveled several buildings. I didn't think it mattered.

"I hope no one you know was hurt in the quake."

"No one," I shook his hand and left. When I got back to the hotel suite, and sat down, I attempted to plan what else I could do. Apparently I was at a dead end at the Vatican.

"How do you suppose he knew about the San Francisco earthquake?" I asked. Everyone in the room just shrugged their shoulders.

"Newspaper, probably," Arthur suggested.

"Go down to the lobby and see if they still have the English reading newspapers from today, yesterday and the day before," I said to James. He left.

"Now, we need a picture of the real president of the Vatican Bank. This man may not have even been him." I said. "Yes, I doubt everything."

"Surely you jest," Chet said.

"Not in the lest. Go to the city records office and see if you can come up with a picture of him, Chet."

"Yes sir," Chet said and left also.

"We will see if we have been hoodwinked."

It was several hours before Chet made it back to the suite, in the meantime we searched the newspapers for any referral to the San Francisco earthquake. There was not a single word in any of them, not even a small paragraph on the back pages.

"Well, maybe he watches international news on the television," James postulated.

"That is possible, but usually they pretty well follow the same news headlines that are found in the newspapers." I said.

"That is true, Reuters News is the main source even for the New York Times. James, call Reuters and see if they have run an article here in Europe, in the last few days about the Frisco quake." I said.

"Yes, sir, I'll get right on it." He left the room to use his own room phone. About that time, Chet came in with a picture of Archbishop Francis. Francis was a different man than the man I met at the Vatican Bank. James came back with the word that Reuters did a small piece about the San Francisco earthquake the day after it happened, but nothing since. It was American news, not European.

"That confirms everything. Well, I'd say, we are being deceived, what do you think?" I asked. Everyone agreed. There was a knock on the door.

"James, that is probably the personal attendant assigned to this suite. Just tell him or her, that we are fine, and there is nothing needs done, please," I said remaining seated on the sofa. James went to the door and peeped out the look-out hole, then opened the door. A young

Chinese woman stepped in and then stepped aside. Behind her came four men who fired tranquilizers into all of us before we could react. I was out.

21.

Chapter Twenty One

The Island of Despair

I WOKE UP LYING ON a straw bed inside a small hut. The door had no lock so I went outside to see where I was. I wasn't bound and there wasn't anyone else around. I walked out to see a sandy shore in front of me. It looked like the ocean, but I wasn't sure if it was the Atlantic or the Pacific Ocean. I looked up in the clear sky and saw that the sun was high, as if at noon, but it was far to the one side of the sky, near the northern sky line. I surmised that due to its location, I was somewhere extremely south of the equator. I walked along the shore, hoping to find someone, but was soon right back to where I started from in front of the hut. I was on a small deserted island several miles across, probably in the South Pacific! My heart sank in despair!

This looked really bad. I had no tools, and no food. The island was so small that there were only a few trees, but several of them bore fruit. One was a banana tree and another looked to be some sort of citrus. That wasn't much but it was better than nothing. That problem aside, my next thought was how to get off the island. I began with the solution, immediately.

I was able to break off branches from the few trees, but not those that had fruit on them. Next I carefully took the long seaweed coupled with tree bark and wove it into rope. The rope held the branches together to form a raft. I was able to fashion sidewalls on the raft, starting in the corners. After that I gathered fruit and put them in bunches in the corners, covering it and securing it completely with woven seaweed and flexible tree bark. Lastly I made an oar out of one of the longer branches. Next I needed a source of water. There was none on the island. I did find an old rusted trash can that had washed up on the shore probably years ago, I scooped up ocean water in it. Next I went around the entire island and found old, plastic water bottles that had found their way to the island. Before now, I condemned the selling of bottled water in plastic bottles due to the fact that they ended up being dumped in the ocean, but now I had a different opinion of it all. I cut the tops and bottoms off of the bottles and made a pipe. I had to use my survival skills that I had learned years ago to make a fire. I then boiled the ocean water from an old time can that I had found, and let the evaporated moisture go up the pipe and condense into plastic bottles. I kept this up continuously for two days, until I was satisfied that my raft could hold no more. I then secured my water supply on the raft. In all the raft probably was about ten feet by ten feet in size. It wasn't much considering how large the ocean was. Before I left, I took the charcoal from the burned wood and darkened my exposed skin to protect me from sunburn. That was important. Suddenly, it dawned on me that my little raft should have a sail. So, I stopped and took the time to weave a sail out of bark and seaweed. I managed to prop a main sail up in about the middle of the raft, and decided it was time to go.

    I pushed the small craft out into the water, and climbed aboard. It was a scary thought to even try to navigate the ocean, not knowing for sure what direction to go. I decide going north would put me in the path of possible ships that travel east to west and back again. That was a good plan, but then, if I was around the Solomon Islands going west may be the best route. I decided to continue north and raised my sail using my branch as a rudder instead of a paddle. There was a good breeze so I felt good about my progress. The wind stressed the seaweed ropes that supported the sail. Soon, I was unable to see the island that I had been stranded on. I wondered where my crew was. They weren't on the island, but maybe they were on another island. They most probably were still in Rome, wondering where I was. I was the target, so they were tranquilized just to neutralize them. I assured myself that they were alright. Day one went by without any problems. I ate several of my fruits and drank one whole bottle of my refined water.

Day two went well also, except I could see sharks approach the raft on occasion. None bothered the raft that day, but the following day, they started to bump the raft as if to test it. The bumps came around more often the day after that, and approached being violent. I decided to take action. The next one to bump the raft got a strong wack with my oar. The shark quickly swam away, but not far. Then, I saw that they started to circle the raft, and I knew then, that I was in for trouble.

One shark would slam into the raft followed by another one. I wasn't sure how much more the raft could take. I rammed the one end of my oar into the mouth of an attacking shark and it got a mouthful of leaves. It swam off. I slammed the next shark squarely on its nose, and it swam off. The rest of them swam away after that. I wondered how long they would stay away.

The following day, I noticed that the ocean waves were getting choppier. Off in the distance I could see very dark clouds coming my way. This may present a worse danger than the sharks because I couldn't scare away a storm. If the raft would break up, I had no chance of survival. I went around and made sure everything was secure and tight while I could.

Soon the monstrous storm was upon me with all its furry! The waves were huge and sent the tiny raft high into the air. Many times the entire raft went underwater. I hung on for dear life. I lost the sail, but the rest of the craft remained intact. Finally, the storm moved away and a bright blue sky appeared above. Everything was still in place! I hadn't lost any of my supplies. The day after the storm I saw a large ship coming my way. It was an American passenger ship headed for Japan. I apparently had been carried quite a distance by the storm, but I wasn't sure since I was lost. Once in Japan, I called my hotel suite in Rome. James answered the phone.

"Mr. Dasher!" he said and I could hear the others express gladness in the background. "We are glad to hear from you! We weren't sure that you were alive. Where are you?"

"Tokyo, Japan. Please get me a flight out of here and back to Rome ASAP. Wire me some money, also. I'll be at the airport."

"I'll do that as soon as I get off the phone, sir."

"Is there anything new there?"

"Nothing that can't wait until you get here, Mr. Dsaher."

I hung up and made my way to the airport .

22.

Chapter Twenty-Two

Playing Dodge the Bullets

I got off the commercial plane in Rome, and I could see my three crewmembers standing at the end of the off-load ramp when bullets started to fly. All the passengers ran for cover as best they could. Being that the bullets were aimed at me, they were a lot closer to me than anyone else. When I made it off the ramp and into the building, the shooting stopped.

"Is everyone alright?" I asked.

"We're fine, the question is are you okay?" Arthur asked.

"Yes, yes, thank you for asking, and thank you for picking me up. I couldn't have done without you."

"The gun shots sounded like they may have come from the roof," Chet suggested.

"Let's go up there," I said. I could see police rushing through the building and then up to the roof.

"It looks the police are going to beat us there," James observed.

"Well, if we go, we may see my would be assassin." I said and we went up the stairs. The escalator was shut off for security reasons. We stopped on the second level and could go no further. The police had the stairs and escalator roped off as a crime scene already.

I walked over to the large observation window and looked out.

"If we stay here, we may see them bring the perpetrator down. Let's wait a few minutes before going back to the hotel suite." I said. Suddenly, I saw a rope drop from the roof.

"Hey, look at this. What is the rope for?" I asked.

A second later I found out. To our surprise we saw Phil Dirt dressed in his suit going down the rope past the window, head first.

"You have to be kidding! I've never seen anyone go down a rope upside down before!" Chet exclaimed.

" Looks impossible to me, but apparently Phil Dirt has it perfected." I said with a smile. "Ops, maybe not. He just fell! Come on maybe we can catch him, now!" We ran down the stairs, and out on to the tarmac. From there we could see him getting into a Jeep that sped off the field.

"Well, he's gone," Chet said. "We could never catch him now. He's too far ahead. Maybe the police will be able to catch him on the road."

"If Dirt is here, Miss Ching must be close by," I said.

"True, let's go to the car and get back to the hotel," James said. "We will be safer there than out in the open like this,"

"James is right, we need to clear out of here as fast as we can," Arthur said.

We went out to the large parking lot and found our car. It was a rather small car, built in the European style. If you want a big car, America is the place to find one, but this wasn't America. Soon after we left the Rome Airport a car started to follow us.

"There's a car following close behind us, Mr. Dasher," James said.

I turned and looked back. There was a Chinese man driving, and a long haired Chinese woman in the passenger seat. It was Miss Ching!

"We can't out run them in this thing. It's a good thing the hotel isn't very far away," I said.

The back glass sounded like it exploded. I turned and looked. There was a large bullet hole in the upper right corner of the back window.

"We can't out run them, James, but try evasive action!" I yelled.

"Right!" he said and began jerking the car from one side to the other. Again, a bullet crashed through the back window. This time it came through the upper left side of the window.

"I'll put a stop to this," Chet said and he pulled a 1911 Browning pistol out of his shoulder holster. He rolled down his window and leaned out. It was a pretty rough ride since James had to jerk the car back and forth. Chet opened fire. After he fired two shots, the car in pursuit slowed down and turned around.

"I guess they couldn't take the shots from my .45. Best gun around you know," Chet said as he settled back down into his seat. "I understand you use your fists and hands as your weapons, boss, but you can't use those all the time. You need to start carrying something for protection."

"I'll keep that in mind, Chet," I replied. I was glad to get back to the hotel suite. Later before bed, I decided to go out on the balcony since there was a beautiful view of Rome from there. James came out and joined me.

"You know Mr. Dasher, this is quite a beautiful city," he said.

"Yes, all lit up at night, it really is quite a sight, I believe we may be at a dead end with the San Francisco money theft. The Vatican Bank may be compromised. Farther, Isaac Levit may be the one who played the part of the bank president, but I'm not even sure of that since I don't know what he looks like for real. Every time I think I have come across him, he is in disguise. The picture of him I have isn't even him."

"He is pretty much a ghost," James said.

Suddenly we heard a popping sound from behind us. I turned around and saw that the sliding glass door now had a bullet hole in it.

Then, we heard the sound of a rifle going off from a distant location.

"Let's get inside! It's not safe out here!" I exclaimed, and we both went back inside in a hurry.

"Well, we just are not safe here in Rome. We probably need to go back to Geneva," James said once inside.

"I came here to get the million dollars back and to capture Isaac Levit. I haven't done either of those yet, so we aren't leaving." I replied.

"Okay, but you are taking a big risk."

"This whole assignment is a big risk. I will visit the Vatican Bank again, but first I will see if you can get me an appointment to see the president of the Commission of Cardinals. They actually run the bank. The president of the commission can open this whole affair up, if he would. We will see if he is compromised. If he is, then, the money is probably irretrievable. Tomorrow, James, first thing, see what you can do for me in this regard."

"You have it Mr. Dasher. Hopefully, the meeting can happen soon.

The longer we stay here, the more chances of one of those pot shots at us will finally score a hit," James said with a frown.

"You are right, eventually the shooter is bound to hit one of us sooner or later, I hope we can get our job done quickly and get out of here," I replied.

"You are posing as a special ambassador from the United States to this cardinal?"

"Yes, that will be fine."

"All your credentials are in the safe if you need any of them," James said.

"I hope I will meet them tomorrow, if everything works out. Now, let's head off to our bedrooms and get some sleep. I know I need some rest. It could be a long day tomorrow."

"It seems like all the days are long in Rome," James said as he was getting ready to go to his bedroom.

"Maybe that is why they call it the eternal city."

23.

Chapter Twenty-three

Going on the Offensive

"Okay, I have my ambassador credentials out of the safe. I have my finest suit on, I'm ready. James, you are going with me. " I said.

"Here, take this with you, just in case," Chet handed me a small box.

"What is it?" I asked.

"Open it and you will find out. From now on, don't leave home without it," he said.

I opened the box and found a small pistol and holster. "You want me to carry this?"

"Yes, it may help when I'm not around. It's a three eighty pistol. It holds six shots and another one is in the chamber. I already loaded it for you with some special high velocity, hollow point bullets. The holster is totally adjustable with its different strap set ups. You can wear it at your hip, on your shoulder or around your ankles. I prefer to wear mine around my ankles. A lot of police use it as a backup weapon."

"I have chosen not to wear a deadly weapon years ago, and never have."

"With all the gun fire aimed at you, you need something to discourage further attacks. As you saw with the car chase, when I started to fire at them, they backed off."

"This thing is pretty small, will it be just as effective?"

"It's not as potent as my nineteen-eleven, but they will get the picture in a hurry once you fire back."

"Well, okay. I'm going to try wearing it around my ankle."

"With an ankle set up, it works better with some sort of high ankle boot. It holds it in place better, otherwise you may end up looking like you walk bow-legged."

"Okay, I'll just stick it on my belt and have it tucked in my pants so that it can't be seen."

"That works," Chet said.

"Thanks," I took my credentials and left with James in our car. The Committee only met twice a month, but we were not meeting the whole committee, just its president. James drove us to the Vatican Gate where we were stopped by the guard. The guard checked our appointment and let us pass. We drove over to the Vatican Palace where we were to meet with the cardinal. The palace was large and stately. Inside we were greeted by someone in a white robe, who walked us to the room where we were to meet the cardinal. The person in white opened the door for us, and invited us to sit at a long, mahogany table and wait for the cardinal to arrive. Afterwards our white robed guide left the room.

We sat for around fifteen minutes, and I began to wonder if this cardinal was going to show, when the door opened and he walked in with a frown. He was dressed in red priestly like gown with a gold cross hung on a long necklace. We both stood went he entered. He went to the head of the table, then smiled and sat down.

"Mr. Ambassador, I am Cardinal John Paul. It is not often that I get a visit from an American Ambassador. From what I understand this meeting is about missing American funds."

"Yes it does, " I said. "The Bank of San Francisco had an unauthorized million dollars wired from its funds to Tel-Aviv, Israel, and then, to the Vatican Bank."

"When did this happen, sir?"

"It's been some time ago now. I was delayed in my investigation by being kidnapped and dumped on a south Pacific island."

"So this monetary transfer of one million dollars came from Israel?" he then pressed a button on his intercom beside him, "Tell my accountant to bring the master ledger in to me, please. I need six months of the latest ledgers." He then released the button, and sat in silence frowning at us. In a few minutes, the accountant, dressed as a priest in black, brought several large books with him and sat them before the president. The accountant stood beside the president as he opened the books. The president turned several pages and looked intently at each. Then, he looked up.

"I see no million dollars coming here from anywhere."

I looked at James, then back at the cardinal. "Is there another book?"

"Another book? I think not."

"Sir, there are other books." The accountant said.

"Well, yes, but the information from those other books are transferred to this one master ledger," he replied.

"May we see the other books, going back six months, also, please?" I asked.

Cardinal John Paul sat for a moment, then gave the command to his accountant to bring the other books in going six months back. The accountant left and was gone for a good long time. He returned to the conference room pushing a large cart that had stacks of books on it.

"Your request may take some time, sir. My time is valuable and therefore limited," Cardinal John Paul said grimly.

"Well, in that case, may we help look for the transfer? It would cut down on the time needed to find it." I suggested.

The cardinal nodded in agreement and the accountant laid the books out on the table in front of us. We all paged through the books looking for a transfer of a large amount from Tel-Aviv.

"You know, it may not have been wired in one lump sum," I warned. "Look also for a series of wired transfers that total a million dollars from Israel.

"Wait a minute, here it is," James said, pointing to a line on a page in the book in front of him. "There are a series of transfers, a week at a time. It looks to add up to an even million. Right here, see it?"

I looked at what he was pointing at, and indeed it was as he said, a million dollars from the Bank of Tel-Aviv. I looked at the title of the ledger book. It was marked as "Special Gifts."

"There, sir, is our million dollars, ear marked as a special gift." I slid the ledger over to Cardinal John Paul. He studied it for a moment.

"You know that those marked as special gifts to the Vatican can not be refunded." He said with a grim frown.

"It wasn't a special gift, it is stolen money. It belongs to the people of San Francisco." I said frowning back.

"That money has already been spent. That money goes to the poor, as well as orphans, and widows." He replied.

"You can't keep stolen money," I replied back.

"We're not keeping it. We don't have it. It is gone out already, and isn't retrievable."

"What are the assets of the Vatican Bank? Billions of dollars, maybe trillions? The wealth of the Roman Catholic Church is a well-known fact. You have a stockpile of gold bars in your vault. You can do something about this money that went through your bank. You can't gift money out that doesn't belong to you!"

"I can't nor will I give out of our funds a million dollars to you," the cardinal said.

"On what moral grounds do you say that? I can't believe that is how you are going to handle this."

"It is not moral grounds, it is financial grounds. A pay out of a million dollars would have to be approved by the Pope. He is the only one who could do that for you. It is out of my hands."

"Well then, we want to see the Pope!" I demanded.

"That would be Pope John Paul the Second. Are you Catholic?"

I looked at James and back at the cardinal. "No, no I'm not. Like you said, I'm here as an ambassador, on financial reasons not moral reasons. Tell him whatever you have to in order to get a meeting with him."

"The Pope is a very busy man, he probably won't be able to see you for months, if at all." The cardinal said. "Right now he is conferring doctor degrees on the priesthood gathered in the Apostolic Palace."

"Do us a favor and find out when our meeting will be, please," I requested.

"For that, you will need to be patient and wait your turn," he said.

The cardinal and his accountant left, taking the ledgers with them.

"You know, we are going to have to wait here for hours, and then, we probably won't get an audience with the Pope any time soon, anyway" James said.

"You are right. Let's go on the offensive and show some initiative. Come on, let's make our own arrangements to see the Pope," I said and we got up from the table and left the palace. "If he is conferring titles and things that may take place in the Apostolic Palace or Saint Peter's Basilica. We will check it out," I said as we hurried along. We found our way inside Saint Peter's with no problem and could hear some people talking down front, toward the altar area. We walked along the side of the large room until we came to the front. There were could see some men all dressed in black seated, some were standing in a line at the front. There was several men, two in red religious garments, and there was one standing in the center, dressed in mostly white with gold trim. He was the one handing out awards. We figured that he must be the Pope. We stood there and watched the ceremony for a long time, until the last person seated had gotten up and received some sort of honor. After that, all those men filed out of the room. The Pope and one cardinal remained speaking with each other in a language I

THE TWISTED CASE OF THE PRESIDENTIAL CONSPIRACY

didn't understand. It looked as if they were getting ready to leave, so I decided to make my move. They had not even noticed us before we walked toward them. The man in red stepped between us and the man in white.

"Hello, I am Ambassador Dash from the United States. I need to see the Pope just for a moment. I promise that I will be brief." I said. The man in red turned and looked back at the Pope. I was aware that the Pope knew and spoke many different languages, so I knew he understood me.

"Yes, you may approach me," the man in white said with a pleasant smile. The man in red stepped aside.

I moved just a little closer to the Pope and stopped. I didn't want to get too close to this man for some reason. "Your Holiness, I have a problem that only you can solve."

"Yes, go on," The Pope sat down in a large, fancy chair and listened.

"Someone has robbed the Bank of San Francisco and has transferred it to the Vatican Bank. It was received as a "special gift." The President of the Vatican Bank has just told me that he cannot return the money since it was received as a special gift. He told me that only you can authorize the return of such a gift. The simple fact is, your church has received stolen funds, and must return it. The people of San Francisco need their money back."

The Pope sat there for a moment and said, "You are right. We will not willingly accept stolen merchandise, including money, as any kind of gift of charity. I will authorize the return of the funds to the Bank of San Francisco." He said. "My assistant will go to do that now. How much money are we talking about?"

"One million dollars," I replied.

"That is indeed a tidy sum, but it will be done immediately. To keep it would be a curse not a blessing," he said with a serious look on his face. The assisting cardinal left immediately. "Now, I need to go. There are things I must do," he said and stood up.

"Thank you, so much. The people of San Francisco thank you!"

"I will have to come and visit there sometime," he said with a smile and then walked out. We left in a hurry also, not wanting to be stopped by anyone who may question the reason for our presence. As we were exiting the building I noticed a man dressed in western attire watching us from a distance as we went to our car.

"That went well for us, didn't it?" James said.

"Yes, now that is only part of the reason we are here. Have you forgotten about Isaac Levit? He is the main reason why I am here. I must capture him and bring him back to the U.S."

"He is quite elusive," James said as we got in the car.

"I haven't given up, James. There are still things I can do to bring him to justice. He is quite the crook you know."

"Right, a theft of a million dollars is no amateur work," James replied. We drove out of the gate of the Vatican and headed to the hotel. Suddenly, our car was bumped from behind, almost throwing us into a stone wall. James was driving and looked frightened.

"Try to keep it under control, James. He's trying to knock us off the road! Look out we have a stone Roman bridge coming up!"

We drove onto the bridge. It was crowded, with cars coming the other way. When we were about half way across the bridge the car behind us slammed into us again sending us against the stonework of the bridge. The driver of the car behind us again slammed into us and we crashed through the stonework and went into the Tiber River. The car behind us also went into the river. James and I managed to get out of the car before if filled with water, but the driver of the other car appeared to have been knocked unconscious by the impact. The river was deep at this time of the year, and flowing rather rapidly. I swam over to the sinking car and pulled the driver out. I met James at the riverbank where I placed the driver. He was still breathing.

"You suppose that is your Isaac Levit, Mr. Dasher?"

I looked at the man lying on the ground, and realized that James could be right. This was Isaac Levit without a disguise!

"You know what, James, we did alright for ourselves today!"

24.

Chapter Twenty-four

Investigating Royalty

THE BANK OF SAN FRANCISCO was so thrilled at getting their million dollars back that they generously rewarded me. I certainly liked the boost in prosperity. Also, I received a bonus from the Clandestine Committee for the capture of I. Loveit. He continuously denied that he was the notorious "I. Loveit," but the shoe fit, so I just left it there. I am not sure what became of him after I turned him over to the committee, since there was not trial of him that was made public. For all I knew, they may have executed him, threw him in prison, or even released him. I had done my job, and the rest of what happened to him was up to the committee.

While I was in the states, I stopped briefly at my office in Clarion, Pennsylvania to see if there was any pressing issues that I needed to address there since it seemed like the major investigation of the Presidential Conspiracy was coming to a near end. Since nothing was on my secretary's desk there in my office I could go elsewhere,. My secretary certainly was glad to see me. She thought I was in a prison somewhere. What counted as far as she was concerned was that her salary was being paid, and that the office remained open. I had sufficient funds to maintain the office along with her salary indefinitely, even before I gained this new lucrative investigation for the committee. I took my crew back to Geneva after that. The day I arrived there, I received a call from Sir.

"Dasher, I need you to expand your investigation to London."

"London?" I said in a surprise.

"Yes, London appears to have had one recent transaction go through Westminster directly from the White House to China . Hopefully, this will finalize your investigation."

"Westminster? Why would it go through Westminster? Anyone in particular at Westminster?" I asked.

" It's royal money laundering by the Queen."

"Oh, that is rich! The Queen of England? You want me to investigate the Queen of England? Queen Elizabeth!" I about fell over backwards.

"That is correct. It is only one transaction, but it is a big multiple one that deals with nuclear weapon's grade uranium, and a long range missile system of delivery."

"Again, you do realize just how impossible this investigation is?"

"Don't worry, you will be supplemented in your income accordingly."

"Do you understand the meaning of impossible?"

"You are Zeb Dasher, the legend. You have done what the FBI, the CIA and MI5 couldn't do. We totally appreciate your talents and fortitude. Now I will send you copies the incriminating evidence. It seems that none of the U.S. government agencies are willing to do much with this. It goes nowhere with Scotland Yard or MI5. You will be on your own. You will receive the evidence in encrypted fax, You will have to take it from there," he said and hung up.

"What is wrong?" James asked.

"I have to investigate the Queen of England, Queen Elizabeth."

"They must be out of their minds!" Chet exclaimed.

"It's surely a joke," Arthur remarked.

THE TWISTED CASE OF THE PRESIDENTIAL CONSPIRACY

"Nobody's laughing," I answered with a big frown for emphasis. "James go down to the desk and pick up the evidence that Sir has just sent me by encrypted fax. " James went and retrieved it immediately. I looked through the four sheets that I received. Indeed, it was a sale of Uranium and a missile system that was purchased from the United States and sent directly from China, via Westminster. The actual final transaction was done on official royal stationary that had the queen's seal on the bottom but no signature. The document itself looked real enough. Why would she do this, if she did? The royal family is fabulously rich, probably one of the richest families in the world. What would be her motivation? Motivation is a major key to crimes. The queen has no motivation to do this. So, my conclusion was that this was bogus. China indeed probably did receive uranium from the U.S. via Westminster but the queen had nothing to do with it. If she were guilty, who would arrest her? This wasn't working out very well in my mind. It looked like some sort of side-track, to cover the real perpetrator of the illegal sale.

The next question was, should I go so far as to prove the queen innocent? Would that be necessary? I decided to go to London to facilitate my investigation. We left the next day. I got a beautiful suite at the Royal Lancaster, London and after that we went to eat at the five star Michelin Star Restaurant, where I ordered my favorite "Humble Chicken" plate. After eating, we decided to take a tour of Westminster for a start. After that we toured Buckingham Palace and lastly Winsor Castle. It was all educational, but Winsor Castle was my mark. The queen actually spent much of her time there, not Westminster, or even Buckingham Palace. I would have to get in and do a search of drawers, closets, and any possible office files that may be there. But how could I do that?

I decided that I would by-pass security. To do that I decided to pose as a member of the Conservationist Maintenance Society that routinely maintains the cleanliness of the entire site. It would give me access to the entire facility. From what I understand the Royal Guard was having some problems with rats, but that wasn't in the castle. I paid my way into the Conservationist Maintenance Society with my Royal Gold Omega Card. The society was more than happy to accept me in as a full member thinking me to be royalty.

The following day I was sent to the castle to join the other members of the society. Several of them were busy carefully taking down some tapestry in a green room. It dated back several centuries and they had to be careful handling it and cleaning it. It was quite a task cleaning the large rooms. I was treated as a VIP member so I had access to most of the rooms, and a choice of tasks. I was to have a mentor assistant go with me to do my tasks, but I asked to be able to look at the rooms so that I could choose which ones I wanted to work on. I excused myself and left the group and wondered from room to room. I found nothing of interest in the first floor, but the second floor was different. I found personal items, including letters of correspondence to and from various dignitaries stuffed in a drawer. This drawer also had blank royal stationary. One letter of correspondence in particular, in the queen's grooming room, grabbed my interest immediately. It had the queen's seal but no signature on it, It was never delivered to the unnamed addressee. It apparently was unfinished and discarded.

It read, "Your old secret is safe and will never be found as it is a museum piece like you. I will never go back to Cirencester to deal with you again. It is over..."

Now, that sounded mysterious in its wording. I stuffed the letter in my sock under the arch of my foot and put my shoe back on. I then continued my search. In another drawer was the queen's royal seal. I thought that was supposed to be locked away and could only be accessed by her for official reasons, but maybe not. Upon close examination of the seal, I concluded that it wasn't the actual royal seal, but a copy. It only had a plain wood handle to the seal, whereas from what I understand, the real one is fancy and made of gold. So, it wasn't

THE TWISTED CASE OF THE PRESIDENTIAL CONSPIRACY

actually the queen who authorized the transaction, but an unknown impostor. I found out later with further investigation into personnel records that a maid named Emmagene Hammond, had access to the queen's things including personal belongings.

I went on in my search but found nothing else that seemed to be suspicious, so I returned to the first floor and joined the others. I selected dusting in the next room as a task. I was given a special cloth and spray for the dust. My mentor demonstrated how she thought it best to do the dusting. I didn't view it as a skill, but I listened to her instructions intently just the same, and did as she asked until the end of the day. We all were briefly searched before leaving at the end of the day. I had to leave a deposit with the society when I joined to insure that I didn't damage anything or steal anything. They said that it was standard procedure for every member, as 11an effective method to insure everyone was careful.

Back at the hotel suite I conferred with my crew. We came to the conclusion that there was something in Cirencester that needed investigating. We weren't sure what. We looked the small town up and decided to visit it on the morrow. It wasn't very far away. Nothing in the U.K is really far away since the whole country is about the size of Alabama. All of Europe is about the size Texas. The British roads were small and narrow. In the United States, some one lane roads are wider than the ones these people travelled on.

We got up early the following day and made our way to the town of Cirencester, Going by the clues of the letter, we stopped at the Corinium Museum. It was a museum that was mostly about the Roman Empire. I figured that there was something in the museum that would give us more information. I and the crew fanned out to cover the museum. I walked over to the curator seated at a small desk.

"Excuse me, may I ask you a question?"

"You are asking one aren't you?" she replied

"Yes, I suppose I am. My question is what were the Roman javelins called? The ones used in battle?"

"Those were called pilums. We have several examples of them off to your left, toward the corner."

"Any books or literature on these Roman weapons?"

"Yes, there is a book over there also that you may look at. This is not a library so you can't check it out and leave with it."

"Thank you very much," I said and walked over to the javelin section. My hunch was that the javelin would be the Roman equivalent of a guided missile. Missiles were sold in the total deal under investigation. There were several javelins propped up in a display case. If I pressed a button on the display case, I could hear a recording about the weapons. I looked at several leaflets that were placed on a table beside the display. It was interesting but I felt like I was getting nowhere. Then I saw a thick book that looked like a library dictionary, but it was on the weapons of war used by the Roman legions. I flipped through it and turned to the section on pilums. To my delight, there were several folded loose pages tucked in the first page of that section. The first page was a hand written note from Emmagene Hammond.

"Loveit,

Now, you see what I have done, I am a traitor to my nation, thanks to you. Now, our enemies have the best, and I feel the worst is yet to come. I will have no more deals. They may come after me soon. Traitors end up dead. I hope you are satisfied,

signed, Emmagene Hammond."

Another sheet was the transfer of four strategic missiles along with a control system. The last sheet was that of the sale of uranium to China. I took the sheets out of the book and tucked them in my front pocket. The queen was cleared of this crime. I wasn't sure of why this Emmagene Hammond would commit such a high crime. She had some motive being associated with Isaac Loveit. I would have to find her to find the answer. Sadly, when we got back to London, I found out that she had committed suicide about a month ago.

This pretty well summed up my investigation. I felt satisfied that I had answered all the answerable questions. I called Sir, and told him what I had found and that I was returning to DC in a few days. I would see him then. He congratulated me on the results of my investigation and that he was looking forward to seeing me soon.

25.
Twenty-five
Investigating the Investigator

WE LANDED IN D.C. A few days later, and we checked back in to the Hay-Adam Hotel. My appointment with Sir was in a few hours so I had time to shower and change my clothing. I planned on going back to my home office in Clarion after that. It would be good to get off of the international travel routine, at least for a while, and just do something that didn't require extensive travel. I had more than enough money now to do what I wanted or to just retire. The retirement idea sounded good but I found out that was out of the question. The meeting was again in a conference room at the Hay-Adam Hotel where I was staying.

"Good to see you, Mr. Dasher, have a seat," Sir smiled and motioned for me to sit down in the chair in front of his desk. I apparently didn't need to be seen by the entire committee, so it was just Sir and I.

"You have done a great job in clearing the President of illegal arms sales and transfers. That part of the investigation has been successfully completed. However, there has been a new report by an informant in South America, that arms are now being sold to Iran via the National Security Council. Your next assignment will be to investigate the allegations."

"I thought I was done with all of this! Will I retain the same privileges?"

"Absolutely. You are covered financially, however I must remind you that you are employed by the Committee, not the U.S. government. Your efforts, if detected by the government, may be suspect. Once again, here is a packet of credentials and information

THE TWISTED CASE OF THE PRESIDENTIAL CONSPIRACY

that you will need to function in your final investigation." He handed me a new packet of ID's and other verifying documents.

"Great, I'm sure all of that will help immensely." It seemed like my investigations for this committee was nothing but on-going. I sought to make this a quick investigation.

"How soon can you get on this assignment?"

"I'm on it now, Sir."

"Thank you," he said and left the conference room. I went back up to my suite where my crew was relaxing. I told them about the newest investigation to which I accepted. They gave me mixed reactions to the new assignment. James and Arthur were somewhat disappointed that we were still doing arms investigations. These type of investigations have proved to be life-threatening. Chet, however, was enthusiastic about the whole thing. He liked the suspense and danger aspect. I, in turn, tried not to let it bother me.

"Well, no matter how we feel about it, it is something that needs done. Thankfully, I may not have to go to South America for my investigation. The NSC is in the White House."

"Great, is there something we can do?" Arthur asked.

"Yes, you can accompany me to the NSC as my assistant. There is a credential in my packet for that. James, you will be my limo-driver. Chet, you are my personal body guard."

"Fair enough, when do we start?"

"Now, we are leaving as soon as I give you your credentials. James buy me a nice, big black limousine, so we can arrive at the White House in style." James got on the phone and made several calls, then came back to the group meeting. I handed everyone their proper credential.

"Done, they will deliver the limo within the hour."

"Great, it's nice to have money. Now, you all need to wear black suits and white shirts. I think everyone has that correct? Let's go folks, we need to look the part. We leave in an hour."

Everyone went to their apartments and changed into fresh, black suits. I left my three-eighty pistol in the suite, since I wouldn't need it for the part I was playing. Not even Chet would be permitted to carry a weapon into the Old Executive Building. I saw that it was an interesting building when we pulled up to it. The architecture didn't seem to match the rest of the D.C. buildings, especially those on Pennsylvania Avenue. Two men in suits stood outside the doors of the building and checked our credentials before we went in.

I had the title of "Inspector General." James and Chet were permitted to come with me. The stately interior of the building looked like a European palace. The flooring and walls were made of marble. In the front hall there was a graceful staircase that ascended to upper floors. Past that was several elevators. This building had five floors not including the basement. We walked through the front greeting hall and down a long hall with offices on both sides. We walked all the way to the end of the hall and found that it accessed a central park area that was surrounded by the building. There was no one walking the hall. I mistakenly thought that there would be a greeter at the door who would have directed us to the correct office, but there wasn't one. Apparently, no one unfamiliar to the building was permitted to enter. The thought came to mind that if I asked anyone a question about where to go, I would be suspect. I back-tracked to a door marked "Records Office" and walked in. This looked much like a library with a main information desk. I stopped there and spoke to the woman seated there.

I showed her my credentials, and asked, "I need to see the NSC expenditure records for this year,"

"Yes sir, those would be in section N, over there. Here follow me." She got up from her desk and escorted me to book shelves with what looked to be law books and ledgers.

"Here we go. These are the present records for this year. They are updated once a month. The new update will be out in a week." She handed a ledger to me, and I sat down at a table with it. I carefully looked at each entry. I found that there were funds to the agency from Iran. Part of the received funds was sent to Nicaragua. I searched and found in the records that the head of the NSC, named McFarlane, had oversight of the transaction. His name came up on a previous investigation. I suspected that it was someone underneath him that was the actual perpetrator but since he was the head of the department, the buck stopped with him. It appeared that a Colonel North who had a basement office, was actually in charge of the operation. I also found what was sold in other records. The NSC was selling Iran guided missiles, which at this point was not a shock. None of this appeared to have congressional or presidential approval. It went through the NSC and then to the bureaucracy of the deep state. It was there that I Loveit finalized the paperwork. It seemed like this sort of thing had been going on further back than my recent investigations. Various people in the government were breaking the law on a regular basis. I made copies of everything using my pen camera. After I was satisfied that I had enough evidence that there was illegal, criminal activity going on, we left.

Back at the Hay-Adam's Hotel, I called Sir, and asked him for an immediate meeting. What I had was hot, and he should have it right away. He agreed to come back over, and meet me in the conference room again.

"Mr. Dasher, you are quite the man! This was an easy one for you. You are done already." He said as we walked into the room. Two committee members were with him.

I handed him the pen, "Here is your evidence, Sir."

He took it and examined it.

"It's all in here in this little thing?"

"Yes, will there be anything else, Sir?" I handed him the collected evidence from my investigation.

"No, not immediately. I do have your number. We will process this and see if we can take action on this. It will be brought to an end one way or another, thanks to you. You will remain on salary, and you can keep the card. We will send you different credentials if needed later."

The meeting came to a quick end, and I walked them out to the waiting limousine.

"I will keep in touch," he said through his back door window. I smiled. As soon the limo drove off, I was jumped on by a man in a suit. He attempted to wrestle me to the pavement, but I was much more skilled in martial arts than he was. He was soon was lying on the pavement in an unconscious state. I turned and two more men in suits were approaching me.

"Oh, the FBI has sent out a couple of their sissies after me."

"You need to come with us, Mr. Dasher. You are wanted for questioning on espionage charges. We will not hurt you if you don't resist."

"Hurt me? I just hope you have the major medical plan the FBI offers. You both are certainly going to join your sissy friend on the pavement."

"Sir, with due respect, we only want to take you to the FBI office for questioning. Then you will be free to go."

"Right. I know you are legally free to lie to me also. I am pretty sure if I do go with you, I will be in prison for a long time without a trial, maybe, never a trial."

"Someone of your stature, sir, will be treated with respect."

"The U.S. government respects no one."

"I assure you that all will be above board, and no harm will come to you."

"You know you are wasting my time. Should I just smash your nose into your skull now, or maybe wait and save it for last on my to-do list?"

"Don't make me draw my gun on you! I can you know since I am being threatened."

"Yes, you can go ahead and draw that gun on me if you want it shoved down your throat."

"Well, then, we will call for back-up."

"You do that and I end this now."

"We will also take your salaried assistants if you don't come peacefully now."

I thought for a moment, and I didn't want any of my crew thrown in a prison for indefinite stays.

"All right, I'll go with you. No handcuffs."

They both smiled and escorted me to their waiting unmarked Crown Victoria police car. I sat in the backseat and they drove me to the FBI building where I was escorted in to an interrogation room.

26.

Chapter Twenty-six

Being Suicided

Without even being questioned, I was taken and locked in a cell in a different building. From what I could gather from what the guards were whispering to themselves, I was to be taken to a "private" prison with an unknown location. There, I would be terminated. They didn't use the word terminated, but I understood I would never come out again, alive. It was a joke to them, but not to me. My body would be dumped at sea along with city garbage.

I was held there for several days before they moved me again to another lock up area in another part of the city. This last time, they put a black bag over my head when I was taken from the cell and transported to another cell. I had no idea where I was. The only thing I knew was that I was still in Washington, D.C. At the new prison, I was beaten on a regular basis each morning. I had no Constitutional rights. One morning, I woke up with a rope around my neck, and two guards standing over me. I was led up and down the hall by being pulled by the neck with this rope. After they beat me, the one guard threw the rope up over a steel pipe that followed the hall ceiling. The two guards both pulled on it, attempting to take my feet off the floor. I am pretty heavy, so they weren't able to do that for long. It was a laughing matter to them. I knew that if I got the chance, they would be laughing no more.

"You are committing suicide! We are here to assist you in anyway possible. Death is the only right that you have remaining!" One of them laughed.

"Yes, and just think of the fine burial at sea the government offers cases like you. There is no charge to your family for the service!"

They gave up after one of them peed himself from laughing. I was shoved back into my small cell and left in the darkness.

The following morning, after my small breakfast and a beating, I was hooded and moved once more to a different location. My guess was that I was being moved to keep my location unknown. I certainly didn't know where I was since I was not permitted to see even a glimpse of the outside world. I wondered how long they would keep this up before I was eliminated. The agents used the term, "neutralized" in such cases to keep it impersonal. It makes it sound like they are not killing a human being that way. Once a person is stripped of their Constitutional rights, they are reduced to animals by the government. I was just being held for the day of slaughter.

One morning before breakfast, the door opened and I was taken to a waiting room and locked in. After waiting there for hours, they opened the door.

"Well, what kind of mess have you gotten yourself into this time, Zeb?"

I looked up and it was Rick Hasselton standing at the open door.

"Rick! Wow, what are you doing here?"

"Seems like some rich friend of yours has paid a fortune to free you. Get up, we are leaving, unless, of course, you prefer to stay," he said with a smile.

Rick's Charger was waiting for us in the parking lot. I sure was glad to see Rick and get out of there!

"Where to?" Rick asked.

The Hay-Adam's Hotel. That is where I left my crew. I hope they are still there."

He took me there in his usual hot rod style of driving and dropped me off at the front door.

"Stay out of trouble, my friend. I'll keep in touch."

"Who bailed me out?" I asked before he drove off.

"I don't have a name, but he had to be filthy rich to pay the price on your head," he said. I nodded and he sped off.

"He's here! The boss is here!" James announced as I came through the front door. Everyone came and greeted me with smiles.

"I knew they couldn't keep you. After all, you are Zeb Dasher." Chet said.

"Yes, I just wonder who I will have to repay."

27.

Chapter Twenty-seven

Paying My Dues

THE PHONE RANG. IT was Sir. He told me that he wanted me to come to a committee meeting that was set for tomorrow. I agreed. The meeting would again be held in the conference room of the hotel where I was staying. The reason for the meeting seemed vague, but I thought that the committee probably needed some details from me about the investigation. With what they have paid me, I was more than happy to answer and questions that they may have or help them in any way I could. Chet escorted me down to the conference room and waited outside the door. I figured it was the committee that bailed me out.

There were three committee members present beside Sir. We all sat down at the table. Sir began the meeting.

"We would like to thank Mr. Zeb Dasher for his fine work in researching all the problems involved in the investigation of the illegal transactions that have occurred between the United State and various rogue nations in recent years. His performance in his duties to us has be above and beyond expectations. For that, we want to thank him at this time. Please stand, Mr. Dasher."

I stood and he walked over to me and handed me an envelope.

"Thank you Sir. I was only glad that I could accomplish what I did. There were many times that I knew only God could help me, and He did. So I give Him thanks, first. Secondly, I am thankful to you and the committee to have given to me the opportunity to serve in something that benefits our great nation. Whatever is in this envelope, I thank you for it also."

"Go ahead and open it, Zeb," Sir said with a smile.

"Okay, if you like," I opened the envelop and pulled out a group of papers. After looking at it, I was floored to see that it was a property deed to a thousand acre estate just outside Boulder, Colorado. My name was printed on the deed.

"Just sign where the x's are, and it's all yours. It's our little token of gratitude."

"Well, this is wonderful! Yes, of course, I'll sign! This is amazing!"

Sir handed me his custom Cross Pen and I leafed through the pages and signed each sheet that had an X.

"Sure is a lot of pages!" I said with a smile, as I signed away.

I then handed the paperwork and pen back to Sir. Sir then handed the papers to one of the committee members who left with it immediately.

"He will have this notarized and give you a copy if you want one," Sir said with a wide smile. The other committee members left the room and four armed men came in wearing swat uniforms.

"What is this? Why are they here?" I asked Sir, as he walked toward the door.

He stopped at the doorway and said, "You didn't read all the paperwork. Inside the deed documents was a confession of high crimes, including espionage, treason and grand theft. You will be openly put on trial for these things, Mr. Dasher. You will be hung, Mr.Dasher. You will go down in history along with the likes of Benedict Arnold, and the Ethel and Julius Rosenberg couple. You need to be more careful."

THE TWISTED CASE OF THE PRESIDENTIAL CONSPIRACY

In stepped Miss Ching through the doorway. She gave him a big hug. "You did it! I am so happy!" she said.

"You see Mr. Dasher, you have been duped. We needed someone to gather all the evidence for us so we could destroy it. We hired the best. You are worth the money. Thanks to your efforts, we were able to cover our tracks and destroy the evidence against us. You now will be the fall guy for the committee, not the President, nor us. Giving you an unlimited spending account was nothing for us, since we make billions. Your spending was chicken feed, Mr. Dasher, chicken feed. Nevertheless, you will have to pay your dues now for that chump change." Sir and Miss Ching walked out, hand in hand. The four swat men aggressively approached me.

That was their mistake. The very first one had his head smashed through the conference room's front door. This alerted Chet who was sitting just outside the door. He opened the door with the swat man's head still stuck in it. A second swat man limply fell through the open door to the floor. Chet stepped over him.

"Anything I can do, Boss?" he asked.

"No, not needed, but thanks anyway," I replied as the third swat man's head bounced off the tabletop. The fourth swat man hurried out the door that Sir and Miss Ching left in. "We have been fools, Chet. What a twist! I have been working for the criminal Deep State all along. Sir is probably the head of them, and he just went out that door. Follow me, Chet! We may catch them!"

28.

Chapter Twenty-eight

Finishing the Investigation

Chet and I crashed through the back door of the hotel only to see Sir's black limousine drive off.

"Where to, now, Zeb?" Chet asked.

"Quick, get the car!" I said but suddenly Rick Hasselton pulled up in front of us in his 1969 Charger 500. I knew we were looking at the right car for this pursuit, because Rick had the best. This thing had a 426 Hemi, high compression engine with the special A833 stick shift transmission. Nothing on the road could out run it.

"Get in, I've got this!" Rick yelled. Chet and I got in the car as quickly as we could, and Rick floored it, leaving black tire marks on the pavement for fifty feet. We roared out from the backside of the hotel and on to Pennsylvania Avenue.

"There they are down there!" I shouted above the thunder of the engine. The black limousine was almost a full city block ahead of us.

"Don't worry, I have this," Rick said with confidence. With expert skill, he wove his way through traffic and passed them.

"Yes, that is their limo with the plates 999," I said.

Sir and Miss Ching did not realize whom it was that had just passed them until Rick pulled in front of them and put on the brakes. Chet and I both jumped out of the car. We ran back to the limousine and pulled both of them out of the back seat.

"You are coming with us, Sir or whatever your name is."

Miss Ching pulled a dagger out of her purse and attempted to stab Chet, but he was able to disarm her in one swift move.

"I'm happy to inform you that you didn't destroy the evidence. I only gave you copies of the documents, Sir. I have all the originals." I told him with a smile. "You destroyed nothing."

"Come on, Zeb, I have some friends at the FBI waiting for these two characters. We have been looking at this committee for quite some time, but had nothing solid until you got involved. Everything that they were going to stick on you is their problem, not yours. Whether you know it or not, I have been secretly tailing you, and recording your actions the best I could. You were on your own sometimes, like when you went to Iran, China and Russia, but I have enough recorded to exonerate you. You have nothing to worry about, you are in the clear. Come on. Zeb you are quite the All-American hero! We are still on the lookout for the one known as Mr. X, but we will get him too, for sure. It's time to bring these two characters to justice. Don't worry about Phil Dirt, either, he'll probably end up shooing himself by accident."

We both laughed as we made our way to the FBI building. I would soon get the details of another investigation that would be unusual and very frightening.

The End

Did you love *The Twisted Case of the Presidential Conspiracy*? Then you should read *The Strange Case of the Missing Bridge*[1] by Dr. Myron Baughman!

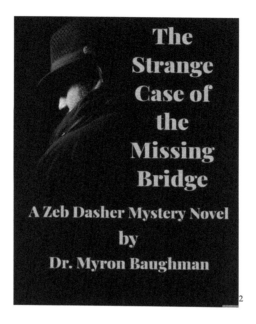

[2]

Zeb Dasher, an internationally renowned investigator, is challenged with a new unusual case. A large, steel bridge has turned up missing, over night in a small town in Pennsylvania. He is called in to investigate the event. Before he realizes it, the case proves to be much deeper than he could ever imagine. He must deal with strange and unusual clues that lead to an on going national conspiracy that could not only end his career but his life.

Read more at https://www.sermonaudio.com/source_detail.asp?sourceid=kingjamesseminary.

---

1. https://books2read.com/u/4A1VDA

2. https://books2read.com/u/4A1VDA

Also by Myron Baughman

Pneumasites
Pneumasites 2

Zeb Dasher Mystery Novels
The Twisted Case of the Presidential Conspiracy

Standalone
Pneumasites
Educating Everett
My Puppy Theo
Trixie: The Pixie Angel
The Ghosts of Griswoldville

Watch for more at https://www.sermonaudio.com/source_detail.asp?sourceid=kingjamesseminary.

Also by Dr. Myron Baughman

Zeb Dasher Mystery Novels
The Twisted Case of the Presidential Conspiracy

Standalone
The Strange Case of the Missing Bridge

Watch for more at https://www.sermonaudio.com/source_detail.asp?sourceid=kingjamesseminary.

About the Author

Dr. Baughman is a graduate of Bob Jones University, with a B.S. in Education. He graduated from the International Bible Seminary with a Th.M. He graduated with honors from the Andersonville Theological Seminary with a D. Min. Dr. Baughman lives with his wife, Denise in Georgia and has four children.

Read more at https://www.sermonaudio.com/source_detail.asp?sourceid=kingjamesseminary.

Milton Keynes UK
Ingram Content Group UK Ltd.
UKHW040256181024
449757UK00001B/73